THE MERCENARY'S MATE

THE BLUE SOLACE: BOOK ONE

C.W. GRAY

Created with Vellum

1

"Next up is a real gem, gentle folks!" The auctioneer leered toward the large crowd at the bottom of the stage. He was a Betonize-human hybrid, sharp teeth a glaring white. "This little girl's part Prime and part Lower. Don't see that on Vextonar too often."

The crowd's boisterous laughter and cheering filled the room. Eight people had already been auctioned off, and the day was still young. Leti Ando gritted his teeth and awkwardly shuffled his feet. The bulky cast on his lower leg made him slower than normal, and there were too many strangers here, too much movement. He wanted to be in his rooms, reading the new Old-Earth journal he'd gotten his hands on.

Draif shot him a sympathetic look. Leti's best friend was no less uncomfortable in the auction house but had insisted on coming with him.

"You knew it'd be like this, Master," Draif whispered.

Leti glared at his friend, his black eye and busted lip protesting the expression. "I hate it when you call me that."

Draif gave him a small smile, dark eyes back on the stage. "I know. Why do you think I do it?" His smile faded. "It's her, Leti."

Leti startled, stumbling and knocking into some of the men around him. He did his best to ignore the grumbles, his heart beating fast. Monty slipped from his head to his shoulder, and Draif grabbed his arm to steady him. For such a small, slender man, Draif had a strong and sure grip that came in handy when Leti's clumsiness attacked.

Leti's eyes locked on the stage. A modestly dressed woman stood tall. She held a whimpering, blanket-wrapped bundle in her arms.

"This little lady is up for sale," the auctioneer said. "She comes from a Prime daddy and his mistress, a Lower woman. Unnamed infant but good potential. Mommy's dead, and Daddy don't want a Lower brat, so there won't be no contest of ownership once she's bought. We'll start bidding at two hundred and fifty? Can I get two fifty?"

Leti sighed and closed his eyes. "I can't believe Father is selling his own child. I hate that he deals in slavery at all, but his own daughter?"

"Yeah, well, he didn't seem to like your opinion too much last night when you brought it up." Draif grabbed his hand and squeezed. "Not that he needs much excuse to beat the shit out of you. It was the threat to sell you too that worries me the most."

It wasn't appropriate for a bed-slave to hold his Master's hand, but the two of them had never been *appropriate*. Nothing was normal about a Prime citizen who didn't have sex with his bed-slave—or treat him like a slave at all—and nothing was normal about a bed-slave who was demisexual with a scarred face and damn good fighting skills.

Draif had been Leti's best friend since they were both fifteen. Leti's father had given Draif to his son and told him to dominate the "broken" slave and prove himself a man. The arrogant Prime often told his son he was so fat and awkward no one would ever want him, especially with his attention always on his studies and research.

Leti might be a breeder male—able to birth children—but his father had assured him no one would ever offer for him like they would a daughter. And love? According to his father, no one could ever love him, not even some mixed breed alien. Being a breeder male showed his blood was too diluted to be human enough. There was too much Wello blood in his ancestry. Father always blamed Leti's mother for it, but never to her face. He was an arrogant bully, not stupid.

In his father's mind, a bed-slave would guarantee that Leti would at least be a man in the bedroom. Leti tried not to complain too much though. Draif had proven to be the best thing that ever happened to him. He was his loyal confidant and best friend from the start and soon became his assistant and bodyguard and a jack of all trades.

Where Leti struggled in anything outside of his

books and pets, Draif could seemingly master any skill if he set his mind to it. More importantly, though, Leti loved Draif more than anything in all the galaxies. He was his brother in all but blood. His family.

"Six twenty to the Drall in the corner. Can I get six thirty, anyone? Six hundred and thirty?"

"Is your lawyer bidding?" Draif whispered.

Leti looked at his communicator. "Yes. He'll keep topping whatever's offered. She'll be ours in a few minutes."

"Your father won't like that, Leti. What are we going to do? We can't hide her in your rooms until she's eighteen. I guess we could put her in Wobble's stable, but who wants to live with an Old-Earth Llama?" Draif paused and eyed his friend. "Well, except for you."

Leti grinned. "When I get her, you are going to take her to the spaceport. Talk with Dottie. She's going to sneak all of us on a random ship going out of the system. Father will be alerted if we use our passports, so we have to sneak, at least at first. Once we're out of the Silverlight system, I can tear up your contract as well as hers. You'll both be free."

Draif squeezed his hand tightly. His eyes left the stage, widening in disbelief. "We're leaving the system?"

Leti snorted. "I've given you several chances to leave over the last ten years, but you wouldn't go."

"I couldn't possibly leave you behind. I love you," he said with no hesitancy. "What about your menagerie?" Draif looked at the vexal newt happily perched on Leti's shoulder. "Monty here wouldn't be a problem, but you can't possibly expect to sneak all of them onboard a ship, and I know you won't leave them." Draif shook his head, dumbfounded. "What about money? How will you survive? I can easily get work, but you're a trained historian. They aren't exactly rolling in credits." He paused, already forming a plan. "I could work, and you could stay home and take care of the baby. You'd be good at that. You love. It's your thing, and, in the end, that's all it really takes. We can figure out how to feed her and change a diaper."

"Ten fifty! Can I get eleven hundred? Anyone? Eleven hundred?"

"Dottie assures me it will be fine. She's picked out a Drellian cargo vessel, and my pets are heading there as we speak, even Wobble." Leti checked his comm, then continued. "As for money, I've been saving for a long time. Do you really think I spend all the credits Father gives me monthly?"

"He's always complaining that you drain his pocket, but I thought he was just being cheap. All you buy are books on your tablet, presents for me, and things for the pets. I think the most expensive thing you ever bought was that tablet. It came from the Anchor's Rest System, right? Our system is seriously behind on tech."

Leti nodded. "I don't usually use more than a quarter of the allowance. I've been saving my pay from my publications too. It's certainly not much, but I didn't become a historian to make money. I never thought I'd have to." Leti laughed ruefully. "I'm a privileged Prime, right?"

Draif let go of his hand and smacked his arm. "No self-deprecation allowed! We are who we are. There's no changing that, especially on this world. It's not like you can change castes and become a Worker. Anyway, the gods know that no one deserves to be related to your father or psycho mother." He smiled sadly and nodded toward Leti's broken ankle. "Their love hurts." He looked worried. "Are you going to pack and bring my things too?"

"Of course! Melinda has already started packing for us."

"Will she alert your father?"

Leti checked his comm again. Things were on track. "No. She's the one who urged me to start saving credits when I was twelve. Once we leave, she's going to go to Rothwell and work with her daughter."

"Good." Draif couldn't seem to stop smiling. "We're really doing this?"

"Fifteen twenty to the gentleman in the front! Sixteen hundred anyone? Sixteen hundred? Going once. Going twice. Sold to the gentleman in the blue coat!"

Despite his worry, Leti grinned. "Yes. We're really doing this."

LETI CURLED FARTHER into himself as he heard steps approaching the crate he had managed to force Biscuit, Gravy, Princess Buttercup, and himself into, along with most of his belongings. Monty perched on Leti's head. It was a bit crowded, though he really hadn't packed much.

Leti was short, but, as his father and mother both loved to point out, he had some extra padding. Gravy, his largest dog, also had some extra padding. The Old-Earth Newfoundland and vexal dog mix took up a lot of space behind him, but he made a nice, gentle prop.

Biscuit wiggled, protesting Leti's movement. The small dog whined in Leti's arms and managed to lick his nose, doggy breath making the limited air that much more uncomfortable. He tried to adjust his leg to straighten out his throbbing ankle. His bags bumped Princess Buttercup's carrier, and a puff of smoke followed his hiss. Definitely crowded.

"Why can't we stay planet side just a little longer?" A female voice rose over the noise of the busy spaceport. It was far too close to his crate for comfort. "I'm sick of seeing the same twelve damn people every second of my life. I need to at least *watch* the dancers at New Hope Casino." Her steps came to a stop to Leti's right. "I hear they're bendy. I need bendy, Alois."

A deep male laugh sounded to his left. "You should have gone last night then." Leti could hear the smug satisfaction in the man's voice. "They were bendy. *Very* bendy."

The crate was lifted, and Leti hugged Biscuit closer, burrowing his face in the long, silky brown hair. If they were caught… He stroked Biscuit's back and leaned into Gravy's side. He hoped Draif and the others were alright in their crates. They needed to leave the planet, but damn, this was scarier than he thought it would be.

"I hate you so much," the woman said. "Unlike some irresponsible jerk-offs, I had guard duty last night."

"Come on, Cordy, don't be mad. I did my best to have enough fun for the both of us." The man laughed again, and the crate shifted to the right, unbalanced. Gravy gave a soft woof, and Princess Buttercup hissed again. Leti cringed and silently thanked the spaceport for being so noisy.

"Hate, Alois. I hate you so much."

"Shit, this crate is so much heavier than the last ones."

Leti sniffed. His extra padding wasn't *that* bad.

"The bendy dancers must have sapped all your strength," the woman said. "Man up, tough guy."

"Cordelia. Alois. Hurry it up already." A new female voice came from a distance in front of the crate. "The captain wants to be off this overcrowded rock within the next hour."

"On our way, Lieutenant," Alois said joyfully.

Cordelia groaned, but they picked up speed, and soon, Leti's crate was lowering again.

"Was that the last one?" Alois asked.

"No, there are two more. Crazy Dottie added three extra crates last minute. Said they were a surprise for the captain. The other two still need to be loaded." She huffed. "No one ever gives me surprises."

"Don't be so grumpy, Cordy. The captain will make sure you get a free night at our next stop," Alois said. "You know he always does."

The two voices faded along with their steps. Leti quickly cracked the top of the crate and peeked out. The cargo space was decently sized, but it sure didn't look like a large Drellian cargo ship. What had Dottie done?

Leti wasn't sure exactly which ship they were now on, but there were literally over a hundred in the spaceport that were leaving Vextonar today and two were slavers.

Despite the Prime's general lack of tolerance for pure alien species, slaver ships docked often, bringing in new species and removing the more undesirable Vextonians on the planet, most from the Lower caste. Leti knew that if he was caught or stayed on his home world, his sister and Draif would be on one of those slaver ships before the week was over—possibly himself as well. His father would be furious at Leti for purchasing his sister and running.

He peeked over the crate again and quickly took another look. The hull of this ship was not massive like the slavers. Relief flooded him. There was no telling what kind of ship this was, but it could definitely be worse.

Leti didn't see anyone in his section of the hull, but he knew that the two strangers would be back soon. Crates were stacked neatly in rows and strapped securely to the floors and walls, and his blended in perfectly. He jostled his ankle and yelped, dots peppering his vision. A few tears leaked from his closed eyes. Gravy slowly sat up and licked his cheek, giving a soft woof afterward.

"Thanks, Gravy. That feels much better," Leti said, voice strained with pain.

He panicked and quickly closed the crate lid when he heard the two crewmembers talking in the distance. Leti chewed his busted lip, then winced.

He couldn't resist. He cracked the lid a bit so he could see the two as they approached. He cuddled Biscuit close, and Gravy propped his head next to Leti's, watching for the two strangers too. Monty scurried from Leti's head to the big dog, and Gravy's heavy panting echoed in the close space.

"Why does the captain only stay in port two days every single time? He might not have to stop as often if he docked the ship somewhere for a week to deal with supplies and clients," Cordelia said.

"You really need to ask?" Alois laughed again. Leti had to admit the man had a nice laugh.

The two strangers came into sight. Cordelia was a tiny blonde human dressed in black body armor. Her expression contrasted her size though. There was steel in her grey eyes and a firmness to her chin. He noticed her pointed ears, poking through her hair. Not quite human like he'd thought.

The other, Alois, was a handsome devil—a Dedril, actually. Leti smiled at his inner joke and then sighed softly. He had a pretty face, and the man was tall—a little over six feet—and well built without being too muscular. A line of dark red scales led out of the top of his black body armor and ran along each side of his classically handsome face. The scales contrasted beautifully with his light peach-toned skin. The

Dedril's warm brown eyes danced with mischief as he helped his friend gently secure the last two crates.

One carried Draif, Leti's sister, two cats, a collection of Druffle, and more baggage. The other carried Wobble, Pork Chop, Hector, and Miss Speckles. Luckily, both crates remained silent. Dottie had sedated Wobble and the others in his crate. She said she would make sure they were packed in comfortably with plenty of air. It didn't ease his guilt. He should have found them new homes instead of bringing them, but he loved them too much to leave them behind.

Cordelia sighed, drawing Leti's attention again.

"Yeah, yeah. Captain Hackett is a big, bad mercenary captain. The fiercest around. He flies across the galaxy, fighting the impossible and winning riches and glory for Charybdis Station. He doesn't need to rest, he is violence and death… blah, blah, blah." She sounded bored.

Leti started to shake, gripping Biscuit tighter to his narrow chest.

Alois threw back his head and cackled. "Oh gods, the captain hates those tabloid stories."

Cordelia frowned. "Well then, he doesn't need to prove them right. We need more time back home instead of all these dangerous missions and short stops. I want to have a real life. Maybe meet someone."

They strapped the last of the crates in and turned to leave. Alois slung his arm around his friend's shoulders.

"We'll get there one day, Cordy. Enjoy the fast life while you can."

Their steps again faded, and the cargo bay door

sealed behind them, shutting out the noisy spaceport and sealing his fate. Leti was so screwed. This wasn't a slaver ship, but it did belong to one of the most terrifying mercenary captains in the galaxy. He didn't think the infamous Captain Hackett would take well to having several stowaway passengers.

2

Captain Will Hackett leaned back in his chair, feet propped up on the round conference table. His heavily muscled, tattooed arms were crossed over his chest, and his bearded face carried his normal scowl.

"The medical bay could really use some updates," Nettle said. "If we stayed in one place long enough, it would be fast and relatively cheap."

Dru, Hack's lieutenant, snorted. "Like the captain will agree to stay in one place long enough." She glared at the captain and pushed his feet off the table.

"Watch yourself, Dru." Hack snarled at the four people seated at the table. Lately, it seemed like all he did was snap at his crew. He had to keep reminding himself that they were his friends, his family.

Nettle laughed and leaned back in his chair. "Maybe we would be able forget that you're all bark and no bite, Captain, if we had more time away from you.

Time apart might make us forget that you're a softie beneath that big, mean exterior."

"It's too late," said Selene, his battle specialist, her voice flat and monotone as usual. "One of his crew gets injured, and he goes into mama mode." She gave him a dry look. "Mama. Mode."

"Umm… We could use some ship upgrades too." Beck's voice was low and deep, his tone hesitant, and he clutched his tail in his hands. The engineering specialist was wedged into the big conference chair. Grell were large folk, and Hack's friend was even larger than most. Muscle, not fat, but still large.

Hack growled and stood, pacing the floor. "We already have another mission, and we don't have time to waste. Is it essential, Nettle? Can it wait until we get back to the station in two weeks?"

"Are we going to stay at the station for more than a few days?" Nettle asked.

"Four days, maybe. If we have to," Hack said.

"Four days? Seriously?" Nettle said, voice rising with each word. "We haven't been back home for over five months, Hack. Four days is nothing. Especially if we have to work on the ship while we're there."

"Ma was hoping to have us all for dinner next time we're in," Beck said. "Four days working wouldn't give us the time."

His big, plain face looked devastated.

"Everyone's tired, Captain. I miss my husband, damn it. Even the ship could use some tender, loving care." Dru sighed. "What's been chasing your ass lately? We've never been gone from home this long."

Hack ignored her and sat, pulling up their itinerary. The schedule rose above the console in the center of the table. Impatience filled him. He needed to be moving, searching, not stuck in place, listening to stupid complaints. Irritation ate at him and he tried to push it away, knowing he was being irrational.

"I just don't see how we can manage more than four days," he said. He didn't want to stay *any* days, much less four. "We have this retrieval job, and then right after that, we have a paid security review on way to the drop off back at the station. Once we do that, we're booked for the next two months."

"We could easily hand some of those jobs over to another team," Dru said. "Yellow Solace would be happy to help, and you know it."

"That's just unprofessional," Hack argued. He jumped up and started pacing again. "We simply don't have the time to spare. We have to stay busy."

"Why, Hack?" Nettle asked, eyes softening with concern. "What *has* been chasing your ass?"

Hack came to a stop, his back to the table. Fuck, he didn't know what to say. He didn't understand this need he felt at all. The irritation and anger with everyone. He loved his home. Charybdis Station took him in when his own bio family wouldn't. His friends here on his ship and back home were part of his family, even if they were annoying at times.

"Hack. Tell us," Selene said, her monotone voice cutting into his thoughts.

He turned back around, facing three concerned

looks and one seemingly bored expression. Gods, he did love Selene and her weirdness. It was comforting.

"I… don't know. Not really," he admitted. He plopped back into his seat, shoulders slumping. "I just feel that I have to keep moving. Have to. If I stop, I'll miss something big. Something important. Fuck, everything annoys the shit out of me too. I can't help it."

Now he faced three puzzled looks and one bored expression. Nettle blinked a few times and then opened his mouth. Shut it. Opened it again. Shut it.

Dru frowned, brow furrowed. "I don't know what to say. What the hell does that even mean?"

Beck's puzzled look suddenly became a smile.

"Captain, you're a Burnished," he said happily.

"Yes, Beck," Hack said slowly. "I *am* from the Burnished Outpost. Thank you for reminding me of a fact I already knew."

"Where you going with that, Beck?" Nettle asked, smiling at the Grell. "Because I have no idea what's wrong with the big lug. It's not like restlessness can be solved with a shot of medicine."

"Burnished have life mates, like the Grell," Beck said excitedly. "Ma always said that right before she met Pops, she got all itchy-footed. It was the mating call."

Dru and Nettle began giggling, then laughing, bodies shaking. Selene almost smiled. Maybe. Hack might have imagined it, or she might just have had gas.

"It's not that, Beck," Hack said indignantly. "I'm not ready to settle down."

Beck smiled and rolled his eyes at Dru and Nettle's

laughter. "Well, ready or not, it sounds like the mating call."

"How would he meet a mate while staying onboard at every port?" Selene asked.

Beck shrugged. "I don't know. I've never felt the mating call. Just know what Ma told me. She said the body knows when your mate is coming."

Dru wiped tears from her eyes, giggling with the occasional snort. "Oh gods, can you imagine Hack mated? He'd expect her to be the perfect warrior and pilot. He'd probably quiz her about the layout of a different ship each day and make her train with Selene every morning. She'd probably kill him in his sleep. Would he even let her in his room?"

Hack frowned. Flying and fighting were important. Everyone needed those skills. So what? It wasn't weird, and, yes, he seldom let anyone in his room, because he saw them enough around the ship. Besides, Dru was a slob. She'd probably leave crumbs all over his floor.

"He never talks to any of the women he fucks now. Can you imagine him with a mate around all the time? He'd probably just growl and snarl at her," Nettle said, still shaking with laughter. "Even when he's in mama mode he snarls."

It was possible, maybe, that Hack had a slightly irritable disposition. Maybe. Honestly, he was surrounded by annoying people all the time, so it was probably not him. Probably. And really, who talked to their one-night stands? The women knew what he wanted, and they wanted the same thing. Anyone who didn't want that, he didn't touch. Fuck, like he had the time or desire to woo someone.

"He'd make her ration out her belongings," Dru continued. "He'd probably only let her have three outfits, one pillow, and maybe her own blanket so he wouldn't have to share."

Hack shook his head and rolled his eyes. The ship was small. There wasn't a lot of space on board, so he made the crew ration out their belongings. It was the only intelligent and responsible thing to do. It didn't matter that there were six empty rooms right now. They might need those later. Even back at the station, he only kept one room since he wasn't mated, so of course, he wouldn't have room for junk. He was just sensible.

"Hey now," Beck said. "The captain would be a good catch. He's a little scary-looking, a bit eccentric, and he does have that weird collection of shrunken heads back at the station, but he's still a catch."

"He decorates his walls with weapons," Selene said. "What woman wouldn't want that?"

"Selene, are you serious or sarcastic right now? I can't always tell," Dru said.

"Weapons are sexy," Selene replied.

"She's serious, Dru, and correct," Hack said. "Weapons are sexy, but it doesn't matter. I'm not feeling any mating call. It's probably just some rare disease. Maybe I'm dying."

The door to the conference room slid open, and Alois and Cordelia walked in, then stood at attention.

"Captain, the crates have all been loaded," Cordelia said.

"Dottie did add on three more though. She said it was a surprise for you," Alois added.

"Aww, she's a sweet woman. Also, a crazy woman, but still… sweet," Nettle said.

Hack sighed and left the conference room, heading for the Bridge. He did love Dottie but not this planet. Time to leave this shitty, caste-obsessed rock.

***

HACK STOOD BEHIND DANNOL, the pilot, and looked out at Vextonar's polluted atmosphere. The planet was basically a large city. There was no agricultural production or natural bodies of water anymore. They had to trade for everything, a fact they relished, seeing it as a sign of prestige. They even dealt in slaves, which Hack detested.

Despite having to rely on other planets to survive, the Prime caste were intolerant bastards. They tended to only deal with the very few remaining species holding at least seventy percent human DNA in their genetics. The purer one's blood, the more prestige one held on their shitty little planet. Hack couldn't stand the arrogant fucks, but Dottie was a sweetie and drew the Blue Solace to Vextonar's port despite the location.

"Set course for Planet Frost Veil," he said once they were clear of the planet's atmosphere.

"Sure thing, Cap," Dannol said, humming happily

and wiggling in his seat. The man was far too perky for Hack's state of mind.

The pilot reminded Hack of a puppy, and he hated puppies. They shat everywhere and then tried to trick you into thinking they were cute and innocent. Beck's ma had one and it always seemed to want to sit on Hack, leaving him covered with hair. Pets were useless.

Impatience and anxiety hit him deep in his chest, and he started pacing again, growling under his breath. He was losing time. He still hadn't found whatever it was he needed, and it pissed him the hell off.

"For the love of catnip, Captain, please calm the hell down," Finn said from his seat next to Dannol. The Cardinal's yellow eyes watched him pace back and forth, and his feline ears twitched atop his head. "Go get a drink or something. Do you want me to ask Nettle to shoot you with a sedative?"

Hack stopped pacing and glared at the man. "Just do your job and stop annoying me. That would help a lot."

Dru walked in at the end of his statement. "Captain, I know Finn is indeed annoying, but no need to growl and hiss at the help." She smiled and smacked Finn's head as she walked past. She sat and leaned back in the captain's chair and smiled sweetly at Hack. "Do you want me to ready a room for your mate? Maybe start a list of items that she'll be able to bring onboard?"

Hack scowled and patted Finn's head. "Don't hit my crew," he said. "And if you keep up with that mate nonsense, I'll send you out the space lock."

Finn grinned at Dru. "Mate nonsense? Do tell."

"Space lock. Out the space lock."

Dru ignored him and told Finn and Dannol about Beck's theory. "Captain here is just grouchy because he's feeling the need for a gentle mate and a loving home, etcetera, etcetera. Beck calls it the mating call."

"Aww, Cap." Dannol shot him a big, soft-eyed look from his seat. "That's so sweet! You're just a grumpy britches because you need some love. Do you want a hug?"

Hack sighed, knowing Dannol was serious. The idiot didn't do sarcasm. "I need a new crew."

Dru cackled. "Alright, alright, Captain. I'll pull myself together." She sat up straight and gave him a mock serious face. "What's the new job, boss?"

Hack glared at her and pointed to the lieutenant's chair. She rolled her eyes and moved as directed. He sat in his own chair and swiveled to face her. "It's Captain, not boss."

Calming himself, he leaned back and crossed his ankles. "We've been privately contacted by the lead scientist at a research station on Frost Veil. His name is Verion Morrick and he's hired us as transport for himself and a package. Apparently, the package is a newly uncovered and unknown artifact. He calls it an 'element.' I don't know what's so special about it, but the admiral has agreed that Morrick can bring it to Charybdis Station to work with one of our teams to study it."

"Sounds simple enough. What about the security review you mentioned earlier? Are we stopping and doing that on the way to the station with Morrick and package in tow?" Dru asked.

"That's the plan. It's on Union Station. Should just be a quick in-and-out job. Client wants a second opinion on a new military division they've initiated."

"Alright, boss. You going to get off the ship there? Maybe take a look at the goods the planet has to offer? Maybe remove the giant pole from up your ass?"

Hack glared. "I hate you. I hate you all."

"Captain, you shouldn't glare so much. You'll give yourself a headache." Finn smiled. "Do you need me to ask Nettle to give you a shot of pain reliever for the ache in your ass? That pole's awful big."

"Leave him alone, Finn." Dannol put the ship on autopilot and jumped from his chair. "He just needs a hug."

Hack groaned and stood completely still as the little Havenite wrapped his narrow arms around Hack and squeezed him tightly, humming softly and rocking him back and forth.

"It'll be alright, Captain. I just know it will."

Dru laughed and Finn took a picture, probably sending it to the rest of the crew.

Hack sighed. *Fuck*, he needed a drink.

3

SILVERLIGHT SYSTEM, EN ROUTE TO PLANET FROST VEIL

*L*eti waited for the ship to take off. Then, he waited two hours longer. Once he was sure they weren't close to Vextonar anymore, he cracked the lid of the crate and looked around the hull. Gravy and Biscuit had both fallen asleep and were snoring, curled up together. Monty was again perched on his head, and Princess Buttercup was getting impatient. He did not like being confined.

"Listen, Princess, you're going to have to stay in there just a little longer. I'll make it up to you, I promise."

Opening the crate, Leti stood and climbed out. His foot caught on the edge of the crate and he fell to the floor, landing on his face. His teeth bit into his lip, splitting it again, and his forehead banged hard on the metal flooring. Monty tumbled off his head and slid across the floor. Dots peppered Leti's vision, but he stumbled to his feet, his ankle, lip, and head aching. He reached back and checked that his two dogs were still sleeping at the bottom of the crate, along with an awake and unhappy Princess Buttercup.

Picking up Monty, Leti lumbered over to one of the other crates and started prying the lid up. He froze when he heard the hull door slide open and a deep voice echo in the large room.

"What in all the Verse did Dottie want to 'surprise' me with? It had better be alcohol. I don't want to waste space on my ship with any useless shit. And why are you all following me? It's my surprise."

"Come on, Captain. We want to see your surprise too." Leti recognized Alois's voice. "Maybe you'll share some of it."

"There are three crates. He'd better share whatever it is," a woman said.

Leti let the crate lid fall shut and rushed to hide behind it. He peeked around the corner just as six people turned into his row of crates. The man at the front caught his attention, and Leti couldn't have turned his eyes away if his life depended on it.

The man was huge, heavily muscled with short black hair cut close to his head. He had dark golden skin that seemed to glow. His ears were pointed but differently from Draif's. They curved up, a good three inches above his head to narrow, graceful tips. Leti didn't recognize his species at all.

The man had wide shoulders and Leti shivered. He loved a nice, wide set of shoulders, and this man carried himself well. His bare arms were covered in elaborate, swirling tattoos that also wrapped around his neck and peeked through the short beard on his face. The man, followed by the others, paused at Leti's open crate.

"Oh shit," Leti whispered. He felt Monty slide off his shoulder and scurry to the floor. He wished he could scurry too.

The gorgeous tattooed man stared into the crate, puzzled. "Dottie sent me dogs and luggage?"

One of the women began to look around the room, while the others stared at the crate in confusion. She was tall and slender with light blue skin. Two gray horns twisted through her dark, braided hair. Her expressionless eyes landed on him immediately. Her head tilted to the side.

"Hack, the crate's open. Something else was in there," another woman said. Mostly human, with slightly pointed ears like Draif's showing her mixed heritage. She was beautiful with brown hair and caramel-colored skin.

Hack? Oh, fudge nuts! He's too beautiful to be an evil mercenary captain.

The blue woman turned to a massive, green male with a plain face and kind eyes. He gripped his furry tail in his hands. The fur was black, just like the hair on his head. The rest of him looked to be covered in fine, short green fur.

"Beck," she said. "How would the captain recognize his mate?"

"For the love of all the galaxies, Selene, why bring that up?" the handsome man bellowed. "Apparently, I now have two dogs and a missing present I already have to deal with. Can we not talk about mates right now? Do we even have dog food on board? Where will they shit?"

Alois and Cordelia slowly backed away from the others.

"We didn't know about this, Captain. I promise," Cordelia said. "We'll go locate something to feed the beasts."

The two quickly turned away and ran toward the exit. Gravy, apparently awake, fully sat up and stared over the edge of the crate, tongue hanging from his mouth. He softly woofed at the gorgeous tattooed man, saying hello. Then he jumped, climbing out of the crate, and sat politely at the captain's feet.

Hackett looked like he was about to have a heart attack. He scowled, eyes squeezed shut, and shook with anger or stress… something powerful. Then he seemed to just release it all. His face grew calm and his body relaxed. His eyes opened again, full of softness and wonder.

"Beck," Selene said in her monotone voice. "Mating?"

The large green man looked thoughtful. "Grell can tell by scent once they've gotten the call, but I don't know about the Burnished. They don't rely on scent so much. Maybe sight, or just being around their mate?"

The caramel-skinned woman looked at Selene in confusion. "What's your deal? This isn't really the time to worry about… *Ahhhhhh!* What the *fuck* is on my head?"

Leti groaned quietly. Monty was the fuck on her head. He must really like her. He usually avoided strangers. Captain Hackett looked up from scratching Gravy's ears and regaling him with baby talk about his cuteness.

"That's a lizard," the captain said. He turned back to Gravy. "Who's a good boy then? Who's a good boy?"

"Get it off! Get it off!" The woman hopped up and down, spinning in circles.

"It's not a lizard. It's just a little vexal newt, Dru," Beck said. He let his tail fall from his hands and picked up Monty, cuddling him and cooing. "You probably need a little water, don't you buddy?"

Selene reached into the open crate and pulled out Princess Buttercup's carrier. "What's this?"

"Stop! Don't open that," Leti yelled, jumping out from behind the crate.

Four pairs of eyes instantly locked on him, but Selene quickly looked away, toward Captain Hackett. Dru had a phaser pointed at him in a heartbeat.

"Hands in the air!"

The crate beside Leti banged opened immediately, Draif pointing his own phasers at Dru, one in each hand. "Put your weapon down!"

Captain Hackett was frozen, eyes on Leti and his hands holding Gravy's ears. Leti couldn't seem to look away from those black eyes. The man was simply gorgeous. He seemed to look straight into Leti's deepest, most vulnerable places, warming him, yet making him shiver at the same time. Something was happening. Something special.

"Put *your* weapons down!"

"I asked you first!"

"I drew my weapon first!"

"You threatened Leti. You put yours down!"

"Listen, kid, put your weapons down and it'll be okay," Dru said kindly. "You're a bed-slave, right? That's what that tattoo on your hand says anyway. We don't deal with slavery here. No need to defend him."

"He's my best friend and I won't let you hurt him!"

"You two are so loud," Selene said, eyes darting between the captain and Leti. "This is a moment and you're ruining it."

Dru darted a look at Selene. "Woman, what is wrong with you?"

Beck followed Selene's eyes and smiled. "Hack's found his mate! Ma's going to be so happy!"

Dru kept her weapon pointed on Leti. "Everyone's gone crazy… Captain?"

Captain Hackett kept his eyes on Leti but absently reached out and grabbed Dru's hand, pulling it down. "Don't point a phaser at people. It's not nice."

"Nice?" Dru sputtered. "You're concerned with nice? Were you not the one who left that Vextonian trading vessel stranded just because its captain annoyed you? Who are you and what have you done with my friend?"

"Draif, he's right. You shouldn't point your phasers at them. We're imposing already," Leti said, still caught in an exquisite black gaze.

Captain Hackett shook his head. "You're no imposition! Really, what can we do to help? Are you alright? Were you cramped up in this crate for long? Do you need food? Water?"

Draif lowered his phasers and looked at the captain in disbelief.

"Stowaways with weapons and you're offering them food and water? Did I hit my head? Am I dreaming?" Dru sputtered. She reluctantly holstered her phaser.

Leti blushed and shook his head.

"I'm fine, thank you. It wasn't as bad as it could have been." He looked at Draif. "Oh, Draif, I'm so sorry. Are you alright? Is my sister okay?"

Draif gave him a wide-eyed stare. "We're fine, Leti. Just being stowaways. On this ship. With a mercenary group. Nothing to worry about at all."

Dru snickered. "Is he being weird too?"

Draif nodded. "He should be shaking and freaking out. He doesn't deal well with change. Doesn't like aggression, or strangers, or people looking like they want to fuck him."

He eyed the captain.

"Thank the gods! I was afraid it was just my crew," Dru said. "At least everyone's crazy together."

Captain Hackett's eyes seemed to joyfully follow Leti's every move and blush, but they grew hard when they landed on his black eye, busted lip, and ankle cast.

"Who the fuck hurt you?"

Leti blinked, confused. "What?"

The captain closed the distance between them in a flash causing Leti to jump and Draif to lift his phasers again. He gently cupped Leti's cheek in one big hand.

"You're hurt," he said softly. "We'll get you to medical and fix you up, but who hurt you? Are you in danger? Do you need help?"

"No, not now," Leti said, blushing again. "We just really needed off the planet, and we had to sneak away, so we couldn't use our passports. I'm so sorry for the inconvenience. I have money and can pay for passage, Captain Hackett."

"Call me Will, and of course you don't need to pay. We're happy to help." His thumb rubbed over Leti's full bottom lip.

Dru threw her hands in the air.

"What the *fuck!* We're mercenaries. Why would we not want money? Let's just help out of the goodness of our hearts! Oh, and call me *Will*." She stomped her foot. "*I* can't even call you Will!"

Draif looked just as horrified, even as he lowered his weapons again. "What is wrong with you, Leti? You're blushing… again. I've never seen you blush so much. Oh gods, did you just flutter your eyelashes at him?"

Selene turned back to the small traveling crate. "Enough of the mating. Why can't I open this?"

Leti pulled his attention away from the captain. He stepped back from the tempting man. "Oh, Princess Buttercup's a bit grouchy right now, so you shouldn't let him out until I spend some time calming him down."

He couldn't resist and leaned into Will's side, enjoying warm arms wrapping around him.

"Princess Buttercup's a him?" Beck asked. He set Monty on Dru's shoulder and helped Draif climb out of his crate.

"Ggghh." Dru shuddered as Monty climbed up onto her head.

Draif laughed nervously and eyed each of the crewmembers uneasily. "Leti was five when he named him and thought he was a girl. Princess was already used to the name when Leti found out he should have been Prince."

Selene peeked into Leti's open crate and picked up Biscuit.

"I will hold this animal then." She looked back at Princess's carrier. "Until later."

Biscuit looked at her, head cocked, then reached out and licked her nose. She set the dog on the floor and wiped her nose off. Biscuit trotted over to Gravy and sat beside the big dog.

"That was disgusting," Selene complained, then walked to Draif's crate. "What's in here?"

She reached in and picked up a fat and sleepy orange tabby cat. Draif grabbed the placid cat from Selene and cuddled her large body close.

"That's Marmalade. She's nervous around strangers," he said.

Dru raised an eyebrow. "Yeah, she looks really nervous."

Leti snickered and whispered to Hack, "Marmalade's Draif's cat. He just doesn't claim her because he says slaves can't own anything. She just cuddles and sleeps all day."

"Slave?" Hack asked, voice lowered. "We don't like slavery in my system. I can't let you keep him as a slave."

"I don't like the institution either," Leti said. He buried his nose into Hack's shirt. "I'm going to tear up his contract as soon as we're out of the system. That's one of the reasons we had to leave."

Hack hummed deeply and sounded pleased as he ran his hand up and down Leti's back. Leti liked the feel of the man's hard body against his own. His soft tummy pressed into the man's side.

Selene reached into the crate again, and pulled out a long-haired calico cat. The cat glared at her and growled.

"How many fucking animals do you have?" Dru asked.

"That's Fluffle." Draif smiled at Selene. "You can hold him."

"I suppose," she agreed. "I don't want to hold the baby."

"Baby?" Beck exclaimed. "What baby?" He rushed to the crate. "Awww, look at the adorable little baby."

Dru frowned. "Why the hell do you have a baby stowed away in a crate? Captain? Do you see this?"

Leti jumped. "How could I have forgotten her? Oh, ducks and chickens, I'm the worst brother ever."

Leti turned away from Hack and looked into Draif's open crate. The baby slept peacefully, unconcerned with the world. She was strapped into her carrier and still wearing the plain white onesie the auction house had dressed her in. Her dark wine-red curls looked just like his own. He just hoped her tan skin didn't freckle over time like his. She was beautiful… and scary.

"Draif," Leti said. "How do I pick her up? I don't want to hurt her."

Draif laughed and came to stand beside him, Marmalade purring in his arms. "I have no idea. She came in the carrier and has been sleeping the whole time. Dottie packed her a bag though."

Dru came to Leti's other side.

"Why do you have a baby if you don't even know how to hold one?" She looked at the little girl curiously, Monty still perched happily on her head. "Is that a slave stamp on her hand?"

"It is." Leti chewed on his bottom lip. "She's my half-sister, but my father wanted her sold, so I anonymously bought her. I'm going to tear up her and Draif's contracts as soon as we reach a different system. Do you want to hold her?"

"Hell no!" Dru looked horrified and quickly backed away. "I do *not* want to jinx myself. I can't have kids right now. We have too much work to do. Right, Captain?"

Hack pressed in behind Leti, bracing his arms on the crate on either side of him. He looked into the crate at the infant. "I don't think pregnancy works that way, Dru. Besides, we could use some time off. We've been going too much the last six months, and I think a break would be a good thing."

Dru, Selene, and Beck silently stared at their captain for a good two minutes.

"What?" Hack shrugged. "A baby's a big responsibility and will take a lot of my time."

Dru started to smile.

"Oh, don't you worry a bit, my dearest Captain." She turned around and headed for the door. "I just have some lists to make. She's a he and has two dogs, two cats, a crated mystery animal, a bed-slave, and a baby. I think that goes over his limit of allowed personal belongings, but I'm sure you'll work something out."

Draif grinned. "You haven't opened the third crate yet."

4

"You had a llama, a pig, and two chickens in a crate?" Nettle shook his head as he sprayed a cast sealer over Leti's broken ankle. He'd ended up resetting it after removing the bulky cast.

Hack shook his head, peeking in the door with Biscuit, Gravy, and Pork Chop piled in behind him. Vextonar was such a backward planet. What planet didn't use the best in medical advances and technology to heal their own?

Nettle moved on to Leti's black eye, spreading micro-healer on the bruising, watching it fade away within seconds. "The captain's okay with all this though, because he's such a nice guy. That's what you said, right?"

Leti blushed and smiled. "Will really is so wonderful. He's not at all like the tabloids say he is. He's gentle, kind, patient, and so damn hot."

Nettle laughed.

"I really wish I had been there." He set the tube

down and picked up the antibacterial healer. "Be careful now, I'm going to seal the cut on your lip."

Leti closed his eyes and stayed as still as possible as Nettle spread the solution on his busted lip.

"I can't believe Vextonar didn't have the materials to do more for your injuries than they did."

After the solution dried and the cut sealed up, Leti wiggled his lips and opened his eyes. "I didn't go to a doctor for Primes. My father never let me when he…" Leti stopped and looked down.

Hack felt his blood start to boil. Fucking Primes.

"Hey now," Nettle said, gripping Leti's chin and tilting his face up. "You don't have to say anything you don't want to, but know that you are far from alone. There aren't many on this ship who haven't been in your position at some point. Charybdis Station tends to draw those that learn the hard way what family truly is."

He smiled gently, eyes sympathetic.

"What is true family?"

"Those who love you, cherish you, accept you, and fight for you. They're the ones who would die for you. The people on this ship, all of us, we're going to be your family, Leti."

Hack couldn't take it anymore. He walked into the room and gathered Leti into his arms. "If you want, I will kill the son-of-a-bitch Prime for you."

He would be so very happy to kill the bastard.

"Will!" Leti's bright smile lit up his eyes, chasing away the sadness. "Of course, you can't kill him. You'd go to jail, and then I'd miss you too much."

"Damn, it's so sweet, too sweet. I may die." Nettle groaned and buried his face in his hands.

The two dogs and the pot-bellied pig decided to join the crowd and casually strolled into the med bay. Nettle's head popped up and he screeched, startling the animals and starry-eyed lovers both.

"Get those animals out of my med bay!" Nettle yelled. "I have to disinfect everything all over again."

Gravy, Biscuit, and Port Chop ran from the room like their tails were on fire. Leti and Hack jumped and went to follow them.

"Thank you, Nettle," Leti said as he ran through the door.

Hack was about to follow, but stopped, turned around, and went back to Nettle.

"Thank you, Nettle," he said and hugged his friend. "I love you."

Nettle froze in surprise. "You're hugging me. Why are you hugging me? Why are you talking about your emotions? What the fuck?"

Hack let him go and followed his mate into the hallway.

"What's happening?" Nettle's plaintive voice followed them as they started toward Hack's quarters, holding hands.

"You look tired," Hack said. "I'll show you our room, and then you can take a nap."

"Our room?" Leti asked. "What does that mean, Will?"

Hack reached his door and it slid open. "Here we are."

He looked around the sparsely decorated room. The pig and dogs instantly went in and began sniffing around. One wall had some of his weapons collection displayed, but otherwise, it was a bed and a dresser. The walls were plain grey, just like the hallways of the ship. He kept his window covering closed all the time, so even the nice view of empty space couldn't be seen.

Maybe Dru had a point.

"So, through that door is the bathroom and the other door is a closet. I don't really use it much. It just has my formal uniform hanging up for when we're back at the station." He looked at Leti's puzzled face. Why did he look confused? Did he not like the place? "You can do whatever you want with the room. We can pick up some more furniture on one of our stops or back at the station."

Leti still didn't look happy. His face was meant for smiling, damn it!

"Anything you want, just let me know."

"So, we're living together?"

"Yes, of course."

"Why?"

Hack froze. Did Leti not want him? Did he think he wouldn't be a good mate? "We're mates," he stuttered. "I thought… I thought you'd want to be with me." He turned away from Leti and sat on the bed, shoulders slumping. "If not, it's okay. We have plenty of space. Maybe you'll change your mind."

Gravy came and put his big head on Hack's knee, brown eyes full of sympathy. Hack played with his silky ears as he grew colder and colder inside. He'd just found his mate, damn it.

"Oh, okay." Leti smiled and plopped down on the bed beside him. "People keep saying the word mate, and I didn't know what that meant for sure." He leaned his head on Hack's shoulder. "So, we're a couple? Just like that?"

Hack breathed a sigh of relief. "Just like that."

"So, where's the baby going to stay?" Beck demanded. The little girl was currently strapped to the big Grell's chest with what looked like a sheet. He hadn't set her down since finding her in the crate. "She can stay with me a couple days if you want some time with your mate. I've already called Ma, and we went over the basic things the baby will need. She's going to talk to the admiral to get you some bigger rooms back at the station and will go ahead and get a nursery set up. She says congratulations on your mating, by the way."

Did Beck even need to breathe? Hack sighed, missing Leti. He needed to stay away from the man for at least a few hours before he had his sweet mate riding his cock. Leti seemed nervous and Hack would *not* risk scaring him off. He'd just found him.

Hack watched Selene and the three men training. Draif had already jumped right in, settling into his room, then seeking out Selene. He was lined up beside two of Hack's newest crew members, Lucas and Morgan. The soon-to-be former slave was a force to behold. He had already blown away his competition with both hand phasers and rifles.

He was deceptively tiny and would have been extraordinarily beautiful without the burns on his face. His dark-brown skin and black hair and eyes reminded Hack a little of the Burnished Outpost, what he remembered anyway. The deserts and golden sands could both be beautiful and dangerous.

"I've started building a crib out of scraps of metal in my workshop, but little Pepper needs stability. It would be good for her right now. Oh, and I stopped and talked with Leti. He's really done a number on your quarters. He was painting when I left, borrowed some paints from Dru, which just tickled her. Your room looks livable now. I've been showing him how to hold Pepper, feed her, and change her diaper. He's still a little nervous, but he's going to be a great big brother."

"Pepper? When did she get a name?"

Beck blushed, cheeks turning dark green. "I just took to calling her that. Of course, if Leti doesn't like it, he'll choose something else. It's his right and all. She just scrunches her nose up like she's about to sneeze all the time, and I do that when I get a whiff of pepper when Juniper's cooking that pasta stuff he loves."

Hack smiled. "Hmm."

Pepper Willa Hackett sounded just about right. He'd ask Leti over dinner tonight. Juniper was cooking some rice dish, and Hack wondered if the cook would mind if he requested some plates in his room instead of eating in the commons like usual.

Wait, he didn't have a table. Damn it!

SELENE COOLLY EYED the three men standing tall in front of her. The grumpy calico cat, Fluffle, sat beside her, glaring at the men. "Now, hand-to-hand. Draif, you're trained in phasers, but I want to see what else you know." Draif nodded once. "Morgan, Lucas, both of you will work together. I want you to attack Draif; don't hold back. We need to see his initial level of skill before moving to vibro blades."

"Sure thing," Morgan said.

The two mercenaries turned to face Draif and began circling him. Draif remained still and looked completely unconcerned. Hack was a little worried. While inexperienced, his men were well-trained, and Leti would kill him if Draif got hurt.

Morgan moved quickly behind Draif and grabbed him around the neck. Morgan went sailing over Draif's shoulder in a matter of seconds while Lucas moved forward, kicking low, aiming for Draif's legs. Before Morgan hit the ground, Draif had jumped over Lucas's kick and rolled behind him, kicking him in the back of the knees and sending the man to the ground.

Morgan and Lucas both got back to their feet quickly, eyes locked on their target. Morgan moved right, Lucas left, the men throwing hits and kicks as fast as they could. Draif dodged or blocked each and every one, spinning and twirling in graceful movements.

"Holy shit!" Beck gently patted Pepper's back and watched the fight in surprise. "Draif can surely move."

"He hasn't gone on the offensive though," Hack mused.

"Can you blame him? Morgan and Lucas aren't wearing their manners right now."

The three men danced around the room at top speed for another ten minutes before Selene stopped them. Draif looked rough. The speed they'd moved at for the little time they had been fighting had worn the man out. Maybe Selene needed to work on endurance with him.

"Why don't you attack?" Her blank stare focused on Draif. "Another few minutes, they'll wear you down and you're dead."

Draif panted, bent at the knees. "Leti's dad hired trainer after trainer for Leti, hoping he'd somehow suddenly become an accomplished fighter since he showed absolutely no talent in politics. Each time, on the first day, he'd just stare at them, sit down at the door of the training facility, and go back to studying for his classes. They wouldn't know what to do."

He grinned, finally catching his breath and standing.

"They couldn't very well attack him to *make* him fight, since he was a Prime, so Leti ordered them to teach me instead. He knew I wanted to know everything about everything, so they'd spend time training me until their contracts were over. I focused on defending Leti, first and foremost." He shrugged. "But, honestly, they weren't too comfortable with the idea of teaching a bed-slave advanced attack strategy."

Lucas laughed. "What else did you learn in Leti's place?"

"Dancing, fashion, and the other social niceties. Then, more importantly, strategy, diplomacy, and financial planning. Leti's head is stuck in history, archaeology, philosophy, and literature. He's smart as hell, but stubborn too. When he doesn't want to do something, he's not going to do it."

Selene nodded. "We know where to start now, don't we? Morgan, begin showing Draif the movements for a basic kick. His first one was pathetic. Lucas, you're more advanced in attack. Watch and advise."

Fluffle nodded to each man and followed Selene as she walked over to Hack and Beck.

"What do you think? He'll make a good addition, right?" Hack smiled as he watched Morgan start running Draif through some basics, Lucas's eagle eyes taking in each move.

"Yes," Selene replied. "Once he builds up his endurance and learns how to properly attack, he'll likely be the best at hand to hand of the crew —even me."

Hack's eyes widened in surprise. "Seriously?"

"He is naturally graceful, observant, and a fast learner. He's already started to mimic Morgan and Lucas during their sparring match, even at the speeds they were moving." Selene looked over the three men coolly. "More importantly, he is absolutely determined and passionate." She turned her expressionless face back to Hack. "Surprisingly, emotion is essential to surviving a battle. It's why I am the best, at least for now."

"Hmm," Beck mused. "You're very emotional, are you?"

"Very," she replied. "It is a burden, but also a gift."

With those final words, Selene and Fluffle left the training room, the cat imitating Selene's predatory stride perfectly.

"Okay, then." Beck nodded, smiling and watching Draif. "He's a good kid, right?"

"Yeah. Leti loves him too, so he'll be on my crew until he doesn't want to be."

"Why wouldn't he want to stay? He seems pretty attached to your mate."

"Eventually, he might want to be his own captain. If he took to diplomacy and strategy half as well as he did fighting, then he'd make a damn fine captain one day. I need to talk to Dannol and get him trained in piloting."

"Can you imagine? From bed-slave to mercenary captain?"

Hack laughed and dropped a kiss on Pepper's head before striding out of the room. "We've seen more surprising things than that."

"CAPTAIN, the admiral called and is waiting on your office line," came through Hack's communicator.

"Thanks, Finn, I'm on it," Hack replied. He quickly walked to his office attached to the bridge and pulled his vid-screen up. Admiral Fasi Juren's craggy face stared back, expression stern.

"Why the fuck was Ma Brakenstone the one to tell me you're mated?" The admiral's voice was pissed, the large purple and white Grell glaring through the screen.

Hack smiled and took his time sitting down at his desk. "Why, hello, Father Dearest. I'm well. How are you?"

"Don't you give me that shit, boy! Who's your mate, and why didn't you tell me?" The admiral's anger seemed to melt away, disappointment settling in. He ran his hands through his white hair, causing it to stick up in wild directions. "I know you've been in a mood the last few months, but were you mad at me? I didn't know, and you just need to tell me if something's wrong, son."

"Oh gods, no! Dad, I'm not mad at you at all." Hack rushed to say. The hurt in his father's eyes made his heart ache. The man had taken him in after saving his life when he was five. There wasn't anything Hack wouldn't do for him. "Apparently, I've been suffering from 'the mating call,' if you're to believe Beck."

"Mating call? Like us Grell? I didn't know the Burnished felt that—not that we know a great deal about the Burnished anyway." He laughed. "That certainly explains your particular dickhead behavior the last few months."

"I guess." Hack shrugged. He really had been a dickhead, not that it was *too* different from his normal behavior. "At any rate, I've met the most amazing, beautiful, sweet man in all the galaxies. You're going to adore him."

His father eyed him. "That is the most idiotic smile I have ever seen on your face. Are you sure you're alright, Will? You're not dying or something? Do I need to call Nettle?"

"Gods, Dad, calm down. I swear I'm fine—more than fine, really—and people need to stop offering to have Nettle shoot me with drugs." Hack leaned back and grinned. "I've never even been with a man before, but I can't wait to get my hands on Leti. His ass is so plump and perfect, and gods, his mouth…"

"My ears! What the fuck? Why would you *say* that, Will?"

"I can't help it. I just feel so damn good. Restless? Nope. Angry? Not even close. Just relaxed and happy. He's in my room right now, painting the walls and redecorating, and I don't even care! Can you believe it?"

"Decorating? You're letting someone *decorate* your room? You've never deviated from stark and sterile even once since you outgrew your Poppy Moppets stage. You loved those puppets."

"Yeah, don't tell him about that, alright? In fact, don't tell anyone. Anyway, he also has a million pets, and I'm just making them space on the ship. Not a complaint to be heard, and you know how I feel about pets."

"Yeah, useless and a waste of time. You wanted one bad as a kid though. Wish I could have gotten you something, but we never had the chance, on the move as much as we were. Once you were an adult, you didn't want anything to do with something that couldn't take care of itself." He paused and grinned, purple eyes dancing. "Say, is one of these new pets a huge black dog that drools a lot?"

"Yeah, that's Gravy. How'd you know?"

"Look to your right, son."

Hack turned and there was Gravy, panting and drooling.

"Yeah, this is Gravy, my favorite." Hack reached over and rubbed his ears. "Isn't he just adorable? I don't know how he got the door open though."

The admiral sat back in his chair and grinned, worry and anger both disappearing. "Well, *fuck me!* You're mated. Look at that smile. Gods, I haven't seen it in years."

"His name's Leti Ando and he's a Prime from Vextonar, but he's not shitty and arrogant like a normal Prime."

"That's good to hear." The admiral smiled softly, patiently listening as Hack went on to excitedly tell him all he knew about Leti and how they'd met. He nodded and smiled, until Hack got to Draif.

"He has a bed-slave named Draif—"

"*What!* Son, that is unacceptable."

"No, Dad. He's going to tear up his contract as soon as we leave the system. They're best friends, and that was a large reason why he snuck on my ship to get away."

"Oh," the admiral said. "Alright then."

"Draif is seriously tough. He's this little guy, but

Selene is sure he'll be able to outfight her soon, and I honestly think the kid will make a good captain one day. I'm going to keep him on my crew as long as he wants though. Leti's very attached to him."

"Hmm. Adding a good one to your crew is certainly a fine idea, but are you sure you're not biased?"

"Selene says he'll soon be better than her at hand to hand," Hack repeated.

"Damn. We'll let your mom have a go at him when you all get to the station."

"Good idea! Leti has a little sister too. He snuck her onboard with everyone else. He bought her at an auction and plans to tear up her contract too."

"He bought her? Who the hell sold her to begin with?"

"His father, but Leti says I can't kill him." Hack growled. It wasn't fair. "He hurt Leti too. Gave him a black eye, broken ankle, and busted lip."

"What's his name? I'll take care of it."

Hack smiled. "I love you, Dad."

"Love you too, son... and there's a chicken on the back of your chair."

5

*L*eti waved goodbye to Dru as she left his newly painted room, Monty perched on her head. For some reason, she had been more than happy to help him paint his quarters, so it hadn't taken very long. She even gave him the paint she had recently bought to redo her own room, white and a lovely dark teal. He really hoped that Will had meant it when he said Leti could do anything he wanted to the room.

"Come on, Biscuit, Pork Chop. We have some errands to run." The two beasties followed him as he left the room and started toward where he thought the commons were. Will had given him a brief tour of the ship before leaving Leti to take a nap. Not that Leti could sleep right then. He was exhausted, but gods, he was so nervous—too nervous to sleep.

Leti needed advice and he needed it now. Normally, he would ask Draif, because he knew the social things that Leti just didn't get, but Draif was training with two of the crewmen, Lucas and Morgan, and Leti didn't want to bother him. His best friend had never been given the chance to make other friends, and Leti was determined to not hold him back. He wanted the whole galaxy to be open to Draif, providing him with every opportunity possible.

Leti needed someone more experienced anyway. Someone who had recently spent time with the bendy dancers from New Hope Casino.

The commons was a large room with several small, round tables as well as a few comfortable chairs and sofas. Leti noticed he would need to add some pet beds and water bowls to the room soon. There were several windows, each displaying the blackness of space spotted with dancing stars. The walls were bright and cheery, and the floors were covered in colorful tiles. It certainly made a change from the grey walls and floor of the hallways and cargo area. Pork Chop seemed fascinated, running at full speed between the tables and around the chairs, sniffing everything he could.

The walls were covered in healthy plants, grown using aeroponics. There were containers with even more plants rooted in soil throughout the room. They ranged from vegetables and herbs, to delicate flowers. Will had mentioned that the cook, Juniper, loved gardening almost as much as he loved cooking. Leti hoped he liked chicken friends too, because Miss Speckles had already made her nest in one large flowerpot filled with greenery. She was settled in the middle, clucking happily, black and white feathers puffed out.

The only ones in the room, Alois, Cordelia, and a

beautiful, golden stranger, sat at one of the tables, sharing a platter of snacks. All three looked up, conversation halting and eyes locking on him the second he walked into the room.

"Leti," Cordelia said, surprised. "What are you doing out of your room? I thought for sure the captain would have you chained to the bed or something."

She reached down to pet Biscuit when he sat beside her, his brown eyes trying to convince her he needed a snack too. She remained unconvinced.

Leti turned red.

"Umm, hi, Cordelia." He squeezed his eyes shut and spoke as fast as he could. "Alois, can I talk to you privately? It will only take a moment, and it's very important."

"Uh, sure," Alois said. He turned to his two companions. "You two can scram for a bit. I'm needed."

"Fine, but I'm taking this dog with me." Cordelia picked up Biscuit and stood. She smiled at Leti, leaning in. "Sorry for being crass. Sometimes I forget not everyone grew up on Charybdis Station surrounded by mercs."

Leti smiled. "No problem. S-sex is kind of what I need to talk to Alois about anyway."

He stuttered over the word *sex*, but he really needed to be more comfortable talking about it so he could get around to actually doing it.

Cordelia sat back down and hugged Biscuit close to her chest. "Now I'm not leaving. You'll need me. I know it."

"Oh gods, he will most certainly need both of us,"

the golden woman said, sitting back down as well. Her hair was a mix of golden browns, shaded from light to dark and pulled into a loose, messy bun. The style somehow looked elegant and graceful while also informal and comfortable. Her skin was a radiant butterscotch, and her eyes were the strangest that Leti had ever seen with no clear pupil, just glowing white gold all the way through.

She was dressed differently as well. Everyone on the ship seemed to wear plain, black body armor, but the stranger wore rich-green pants and a flowing, green-and-gold tunic. She looked both fashionable and functional, standing out from the others around her.

"What's this, now?" Alois asked. "Leti clearly came to me for advice, and you two don't need to poke your noses in it."

"If it's about sex, yes we do. You certainly can't be trusted to give advice on *relationship* sex." The golden woman shot back. "By the way, dear, I'm Ava. We haven't met yet. I mostly deal with the diplomatic needs on our missions." She gestured to the last chair at the small table. "Take a seat, and let's figure out what you need, sweetie."

Leti sat, nervously tapping his foot.

Ava reached over and grabbed his hand, smiling brightly. "Now, what's wrong? I've heard how you and the captain couldn't take your eyes off one another when you met. Why are you so nervous now?"

"Um… well… when I was hidden, I overheard Alois and Cordelia talking about the dancers from New Hope Casino."

Cordelia laughed. "Sorry about that, Leti. Not that I can promise I wouldn't have said the same things even if I *had* known you were there."

Alois smiled and leaned back in his chair. "Good memories."

"Yes, I'm sure. Um, okay, I can do this," Leti said, nose scrunching up. He put on his determined face, then growled softly. There, see how determined he was. He wiggled in his seat, trying to ignore Cordelia's laughter.

"That was the cutest little growl," Cordelia said, giggling. Alois's eyes widened and his lips clamped together. He looked to be trying to hold back his own laughter.

Ava smiled sweetly. "Of course, you can do this, honeypot. Please, feel free to say anything you like. Ask anything."

"So, I haven't really had much experience with sex, and since Alois clearly has, I thought he might be able to give me some pointers."

"Well, he does have experience," Cordelia said dryly.

"Yes, he's a man whore." Ava nodded. "He very well could explain the basics, but remember that sex is more than just movements and where to put what."

"I can definitely help, Leti." Alois grinned. "You came to the right person. Just ignore these two. Sex is all about movement." He flicked a carrot across the table at Ava. "Now, exactly how much experience do you have? What's our starting point?"

"Well, that would be *no* experience... at all. Our starting point would be zero."

Alois nodded thoughtfully. "Okay, so no sex? Anything? Hand job or blow job?"

"That would be a solid no to all of it."

"Why the hell not?" Cordelia asked. The other two glared at her.

"You may have noticed, but I'm not an attractive person." Leti chewed his lip nervously and gestured to his belly. "I'm fat and I have all these freckles."

The three mercenaries stared at him in silence for several minutes, making him even more nervous. "Bullshit," Alois finally said. "I call bullshit."

"I second the call of bullshit," Cordelia said, frowning.

"I'm afraid to say it, but I agree with these two," Ava added. "I third the call of bullshit. How could you possibly think you're unattractive? Fat?"

"Have you not seen your ass?" Cordelia jumped out of her seat and set Biscuit down. She pulled Leti out of his own seat and spun him around. His butt pointed toward the table. Could mortification kill a person? He thought it might.

"Look at this ass! Alois, you would fuck this ass, right?" Cordelia gestured to Leti's butt with both hands, like it was a prize in a gameshow.

"Yes… Yes, I would." Alois nodded, face serious. "Except the captain would murder me in a very slow and painful manner."

"Your bottom is especially lovely, Leti," Ava added. "Really, love bug, when you add in your adorable freckles, I can't possibly imagine how you could think you're unappealing to anyone, much less your mate."

Leti quickly turned back around, a strange warmth spreading through him. Maybe he wasn't hideous like his father and mother had said. Maybe he could entice Will to be with him forever and ever. These people had no reason to lie to him, and they weren't family like Draif. Will had to say Leti was beautiful. Love required it.

"Plus, a little extra padding is surely not a bad thing." Alois leered. "You have curves and a softness that would be perfect to hold, little man… If you didn't belong to the captain." His gaze turned predatory. "Say, are you freckled all over? Just curious."

Cordelia snorted and slapped Alois's arm.

"Hush, you. Gods, Leti, all of that's not even considering your personality," Cordelia said. "I know we don't know one another well, but all your pets? That takes a lot of love and patience."

"Sugarplum, you left a privileged life of leisure to offer better lives to your best friend and little sister," Ava said.

Apparently, information travels fast on a spaceship, Leti thought.

"Fuck, man. You're raising your little sister. A lot of people wouldn't do that even if it didn't involve picking up and shipping off planet." Alois's voice turned bitter. "Family doesn't mean unconditional love to everyone."

Leti sat. "My life was really very easy to leave behind, so don't go thinking I'm some kind of hero." He smiled gently at Alois. "You're right about family though. Of course, I'm avoiding my sister right now. She scares me to death, but I love her completely. I'll do anything for her. Not everyone gets it, but I see you all. I know you're each other's family. You all belong to Will, and that means you'll be my family too. I'm not so special; I'm just like you all. Now, I appreciate the compliments. I think you're all crazy, but that seems to be the norm here. So, tell me, what can I do to seduce Will?"

"Now we're talking," Alois crowed.

"First, darling," Ava said. "We do need to talk about your clothes." She gestured to his shirt. "While it's simply adorable and suits you, a sweater with penguins on it isn't considered seductive."

"But it's cold in space..." He pouted. "And I like penguins."

Cordelia chortled. "It's not like the captain's going to keep him in clothes for long anyway."

"Still, presentation is important," Ava said.

"Ugh, you all are turning something very simple into a complicated mess." Alois groaned.

"Let's go back to your quarters and see what we have to work with," Ava said.

"Okay, but the room doesn't really have seats yet. Do you all mind sitting on the floor?"

"Whoa, let's makes some stops on the way," Cordelia said. "I don't know about presentation, but the more surfaces in the room, the more places to fuck."

"Goodness, Cordy," Ava said and sighed. "You do need more furniture though. How the captain thought the room didn't need at least one chair, I don't understand."

Alois pulled Leti from his seat, and the foursome

quickly exited the commons followed by Biscuit. Pork Chop had already taken over a large, comfortable-looking chair near the kitchen entrance. He snuffled in his sleep and began to snore.

Stopping by each crew member's quarters to grab things, they eventually made it to Leti and Will's room, arms overflowing.

Setting everything down on the bed, Alois stretched his back and looked around. "Nice walls, but yeah, it's a bit bare in here."

"I'll go grab Finn and Beck and make them help me round up some furniture," Cordelia said. "Do you want a desk, Leti? What about tech? Do you at least have a tablet? I know Vextonar's not the most advanced planet in the world."

Leti looked up from rooting through all his new stuff. Each member of the crew had been very generous, and it was special because it all came from Will's family. "I have a tablet, but nothing else. Draif doesn't have anything, and I know he'd really like the access if it's possible."

"On it," Cordelia said and ran out the door, Biscuit racing at her heels.

"Alois, start laying down these rugs. We'll make up the bed once we've emptied it of all this stuff. I really didn't realize everyone had so much on board. I guess I wasn't the only one who ignored the captain's stupid restrictions about personal belongings," Ava said.

"I have some things too, from home." Leti gestured toward the bathroom. "I stashed it all in there while we were painting. I have my collection of Druffle too."

"Druffle?" Ava looked curious. "Aren't they those little fuzzball creatures?"

"Yes," Leti answered and opened the bathroom door. "See? Aren't they cute?"

His Druffle were overflowing a large, segmented container. The top was see-through and allowed the Druffle space to crawl around, with little ramps and wheels. The bottom was closed off for privacy, offering them quiet places to sleep. They were active now, running up and down ramps and racing on their wheels.

Ava gasped and squealed. "I need some. I need some Druffle right now."

Leti laughed. "When we land somewhere that has them, I'll get you a Druffle stand and split mine with you. It's getting a little crowded for them anyway."

Ava squealed again and hugged him tightly. "Thank you!" She took a breath and shook off her excitement. "Alright now, did you bring clothes with you too?"

"Mostly I packed my favorite blankets—I collect them too—but I did bring some clothes."

"Oh, good. Start modeling your sexy clothes for us, buttercup," Ava said, going back into the room and pulling a large folding screen off the bed, placing it in the far corner.

"*What?*" Leti folded his arms over his chest, like he was hiding his bare body from view. "I don't have sexy clothes… unless sweaters are sexy."

"If all you're wearing is the sweater…"

"Oh, do hush, Alois," Ava said. "Let me think." She looked up and down Leti's body and hummed. "I think

I might have something. The captain's not going to know what hit him." She darted toward the door. "Be right back!"

"Gods, finally, they're gone." Alois plopped down on the floor and patted the spot in front of him. "Come on, Leti. Have a seat."

"Okay." Leti sat, facing Alois, curious about what the man wanted.

"Before they get back, we need to have 'the talk.'" He patted Leti's crossed leg. "Sex for the first time can definitely be scary, but honestly, none of us are born knowing how to be great lovers. It's all about learning and experimenting until you become comfortable. Now, my first bit of advice is to not rush straight to penetration. Take your time and start with what feels good. Nothing you do will make the captain unhappy. He's your mate, and he is fast on the way to loving you. I've never seen him smile the way he does around you."

Leti was shocked, mouth hanging open. He'd expected Alois to jump straight to talking about different positions. This was actually far more comforting.

"So, first and most importantly, when you are ready for penetration, make sure you take time to get ready. He needs to make you as aroused as possible, instead of diving right in. The captain should know this, but just in case. Also, you can top him too. Don't be afraid to switch it up, and don't feel like you have to fit some stupid stereotype. Yes, you're the smaller guy, but it doesn't automatically mean you need to be the bottom.

Do what feels best to you and your partner, not what you think people expect."

Gods, Leti had never thought of being the one doing the penetrating. *Interesting.*

"Now, my second bit of advice is to be an active participant. Don't be passive. Touch him. Explore him. Remember, nothing you do is likely to send him running. Just like you need to be fully aroused and ready when the time comes for penetration, so does he."

Leti couldn't just lie there and let Will do all the work? While he wouldn't mess up that way, he guessed it did sound boring. At least he'd get to touch and taste, and that was certainly a benefit.

"Lots of men would say: just watch some porn and you'll get it. But if you go that route, Leti, please by the gods, don't just try to do what you see the actors do. First, while porn has its place, it's not realistic, and secondly, what works for some people may not work for you and the captain. It all goes back to the beginning with focusing on what you're comfortable with and what feels good. You can branch off from there and I guarantee it will be a better experience."

Leti had never, and would never, watch porn. He would die of embarrassment.

"Finally, once you've been with the captain a million times, so probably by next week, remember to not become complacent. Revel in the anticipation, have sex in different places, and try different positions. But first, spend that time getting comfortable in your own skin and make sure to pay attention to your partner. Tell him what you like, and what you don't like. Tell him you care about him." Alois paused and looked carefully at Leti. "Listen to him. Not just his words but his body. What does he like? What doesn't he like? The captain will do whatever you ask him to, but it's your job to make sure he enjoys it. Just like it's his job to make sure you enjoy it." Alois patted his leg again. "Any questions? I know I didn't start listing positions, but I promise, this stuff is much more important."

The door opened and Ava rushed in, arms full of clothing. She paused at the sight of them, raising one golden brown eyebrow. "Please tell me Alois isn't filling your head with nonsense?"

Alois stood and bowed toward Ava. "Nonsense is my specialty, Ava love."

Leti stood too and hugged a surprised Alois. "Thank you, Alois. I really appreciate your help. I feel much better about tonight."

Ava gaped, and Alois's face softened from its normal arrogant expression. He hugged Leti back tightly. "No problem, Leti. You need anything, you let me know. The captain is a lucky man."

Ava grinned and started laying out outfits. "Come along, lovely boy. I have some ideas on an outfit for tonight."

6

When Hack and Gravy stopped by his room to pick up Leti for dinner, he opened the door, then turned to leave, thinking it was someone else's room.

"Will?" Leti's voice called out. "Where are you going? Do you not like the changes I made?"

He sounded nervous and sad. That was unacceptable.

Hack turned back around and entered the room again. It was completely changed from the cold, sterile place he had long grown used to. The walls were painted white and teal, and the large window was uncovered, revealing an approaching planet.

The cold grey floor was covered with a myriad collection of rugs in bright, bold blues, greens, purples, and reds. Dotted throughout the room were soft, plush chairs, pet beds, and pet toys. Gravy instantly went to a large purple pet bed and plopped down, huffing.

An intricately framed screen hid a corner of the

room from view, and a desk loaded up with the latest technology sat across from the bed. Behind it, on the wall, was a large vid-screen that hadn't been there before. On either side of it, his weapons collection was spread out, intermingled with other objects. There were a few masks, a short tapestry, ancient farming tools, and artifacts he didn't recognize. All around the room hung long, trailing, colorful plants and Hack recognized Juniper's work.

In another corner was Leti's collection of Druffle, their container bolted to the wall. Several tunnels branched off from the original container, winding in different directions across the closest wall, telling him that Beck had been hard at work all afternoon. Druffle ran throughout the tunnels, exploring their new territory.

His grey and white bed was completely different now, welcoming and warm. The deep-purple-and-blue blanket was partially covered with small, soft, multi-colored patterned blankets. What seemed like a million pillows lined the top. Above the bed, a large, boldly colored painting of a nature scene hung, brushstrokes blurred. It looked suspiciously like one that Morgan had fallen in love with a few planets back.

Against the wall, under the window, was a small table with two chairs. Next to it stood the most beautiful sight in the entire room. Leti moved nervously from foot to foot next to the table. His soft, sweet body was covered with a filmy gold robe that offered shadowed peeks beneath it.

"Juniper brought dinner a few minutes ago. He's a

really nice guy, even if he stole Miss Speckles and Pork Chop."

"That's nice," Hack said, distracted. "What's that you're wearing, Leti?" He prowled closer to his mate, pulling him into his arms. Leti's soft body fit perfectly against his hard one.

Leti snuggled closer, tilting his head back and settling a small kiss on the bottom of Hack's jaw. "Ava gave me this robe she bought on Haven. Do you like it? I didn't think I would because it's so froufrou, but it's really comfortable. I may wear it all the time."

"I think that's a good idea, as long as no one else sees you in it. My crew doesn't need to get any ideas about stealing my mate."

Leti laughed. "Okay, boss."

"Oh gods, you've been around Dru too much already."

"Alois, Cordy, and Ava too."

"You're ruined!" Hack laughed and reluctantly stepped away from his mate. He pulled a chair back. "Ready for dinner?"

Leti smiled and sat. "It smells so good. I could never pick up cooking. I tried, because it annoyed Mother, but it was no use. Draif took to it though. His Punjabi chicken is *really* good, but don't tell Hector or Miss Speckles I said that."

"I'm starting to see that Draif is scarily efficient at everything," Hack said, smiling. "I think he'll make a good mercenary captain one day if he wants it bad enough."

Leti's smile beamed across the table. "I'm so glad

you noticed. Everyone overlooks Draif because he's a slave, but he is so much more than that. I can't wait until I get to tear up his contract."

"Me too. I hope you don't mind, but I've already asked him to join the crew. He said as long as you're on board, he'll be too."

"That's great, and maybe not great too. I hope he doesn't stick to solely protecting me like he did back home. It's not that I mind—I enjoy him being close— but I want him to grow, maybe become his own captain one day like you said." Leti sighed, spooning up another mouthful of rice casserole. "I don't want to hold him back."

"I'll keep pushing him to learn new things, but you don't hold him back. I think you've held him together for a long time. He'll realize he can stand on his own soon enough."

"You're right, I know. I just worry." Leti shook his head. "Anyway, Beck has my sister for the night. Did you know he named her Pepper? I love it!"

"He mentioned it earlier. I was thinking Pepper Willa Hackett had a nice ring to it. Her birth certificate still needs to be filed and we can do that after tearing up her contract, file her as a freewoman. Saves some time."

"Pepper Willa Hackett, huh?" Leti grinned and laughed. "It sounds perfect."

"Like Leti Hackett does?"

"We'll see, boss man, but we're in no rush. Now, you know my family, and I know your crew, but do you have any family back at Charybdis Station? I don't know anything about the Burnished."

"I don't know much myself, just a few of the basics from when I was a kid." Hack shrugged. He hated talking about his past, but this was his mate. "Burnished Outpost is the only planet in the Anchor's Rest System that keeps completely to itself. The people are nomadic, led by a chief, and the planet is mostly desert. I remember traveling in a caravan with my mother, father, and grandparents. I think I remember cousins too, but it's been so long ago."

"If it's hard to talk about, you don't have to, Will. I want to know everything about you, but I don't want to hurt you by having you recall painful memories."

Hack looked up from his plate. Leti's concerned expression eased his discomfort. "It's okay. I haven't told anyone else everything that happened, but you're my mate, right? Who better to share my memories with?"

"Yes." Leti nodded. "I would be honored to hold your memories, good or bad."

Hack nodded and began. "When I was five, my father died. That is the worst memory. He loved me, taught me how to find my fire."

"Your fire? What's that mean?"

"Fire is revered on Burnished Outpost. It's not well-known, but the Burnished are born with their tattoos. These aren't ink." Hack held his bare arm up. The black patterns seemed to twist and twirl, moving for a moment before going still again. "Some of us can call fire through them, but it's hard, and you have to be properly trained to control it or you'll burn to a crisp."

"That's amazing," Leti said, tracing the pattern on Hack's hand. "Do you use it often?"

"Yeah. When we're fighting hand to hand, it can be pretty useful."

"Your father taught you how to control it? How old were you?"

"I was four when I started feeling it. He'd only just finished training me in the basics when he died. I was five." He sighed and closed his eyes. "The Burnished are really particular about survival. I can remember that much. If someone can't survive on their own, then they're left for dead at a special spot, given up to the gods.

"The Burnished hunt for survival, seeing life as a test of a person's mettle. Easy isn't what they want, and they hold tight to their traditions, good or bad. It's an odd place, a mixture of technology and barbarism. Humans didn't do too well when they settled there, but the stronger ones mated with the native Burnished. Strength was what was important, not species."

He opened his eyes, focusing on his mate. "My father was different though. I remember him trying to make things easier for everyone, trying new methods of hunting. He even wanted to raise orilleos, a type of wild herd animal. Said we could eat more that way. The other men and women in the tribe didn't like the idea of change. I remember them coming to our tent that night, yelling, pulling my father away. I remember the fire, the stench of burning flesh and his screams. My mother just sat there and watched. She didn't fight them, just held me back and watched."

"Oh gods…" Leti's look of horror urged Hack on. He had to tell it all.

"With my father dead, my mother couldn't take care of both me and herself. I remember her bringing me to each of my family members, some are clear as day and some I can barely picture. My grandparents, both sets, refused to care for me. I remember that. I remember hunting with Grandpa Moses and Grandpa Solis before that day, the fun we had. They'd hugged me and smiled with pride after I caught my first rabbit when I was three, but the way they looked at me that day though? It hurt. The way my father died made him weak in their eyes, dishonorable. Me being his son? That made *me* weak, and I could see their hatred right there on their faces."

Leti grabbed his hand and squeezed tightly, face filled with both sympathy and anger.

"My mother took me to each and every family member, but like I said, I don't remember them all. They all refused though. So, my mother took me to Dead Ridge. It was one of the highest dunes in the largest desert and where the weak were left. It took days to get there, and she didn't share any of her food or water with me. She didn't talk either. I asked question after question, but she just ignored me. I caught a rabbit or two, but I couldn't find much water. When we got there, we made camp and I went to sleep. I don't think I've ever been so tired. When I woke up, she was gone, all our belongings gone with her. She didn't even leave my sling."

"Will," Leti said, tears pooling in his eyes.

"I stayed there for at least a full day, waiting for her to come back, unwilling to believe she'd left me to die. What I didn't know was that Charybdis Station sends a patrol to fly over Dead Ridge once a day, every day. They use it as a training exercise and pick up any person that's been left there. I don't know if my mother knew or not. I don't even know if the Burnished chief knew they did it. In any case, a new recruit named Fasi Juren, a Grell, found me that day."

Hack smiled, filling him "He had just gotten married, but he convinced his wife, Renee, that they needed to adopt me. It didn't take much convincing, just one video call. I remember waving hello while I stuffed my face with his rations. When he landed at the station and carried me to Medical, she was already there in her brand-new security uniform, carrying this huge stuffed wolf."

"Did they love you, Will?"

Hack laughed. "Yes, they did and still do. What's more, I got two new brothers out of it along with the best parents anyone could have. Except Beck. His Ma and Pops are equal to mine, but that's it. No other parents can compete."

Leti's smile faded. "I'm not a violent person, Will," he said, standing and moving toward him.

"Okay?" Hack frowned. Leti gently sat in his lap, moving around to get comfortable.

"While I don't like the idea of hurting someone in

general, Will, let me be clear." Leti placed his hands on each side of Hack's face, his eyes fierce. "I would fight for you," he said. "If someone tried to take you from me, I would scream, kick, hit, and bite, anything I could do. They would have to drag me away too, and I would fight them with everything I have."

"Leti..."

"I know we don't fully know one another yet, but, Will, I will never leave you. I will never abandon you, even if it means I die along with you. I don't leave my loved ones behind." He gently kissed Hack's lips, salt from his tears mixing with his taste.

"You're mine, Leti..." Hack whispered against his lips, heart full. "And I'm yours." He deepened their kiss, tongue delving inside. He wrapped his arms around Leti's soft body, pulling him close, bumping the table. He pulled his lips from Leti's. "Come on, let's move to the bed."

Hack lifted Leti, his mate squeaking and wrapping his arms around Hack's neck in surprise. A few steps later and he gently placed his mate on their bed, quickly lying down next to him to continue their kiss. His hand smoothed across Leti's hip, gripping tightly and pulling him closer. His mate's hard length pressed into his stomach, fueling the fire spreading through Hack. He had waited for this moment since the second he'd laid eyes on Leti.

Leti's hands didn't remain still. He stroked across Hack's shoulders, chest, then down his abdomen, hands warm even through Hack's clothes. He pushed Hack to his back and lay over him, his kisses inexperienced but sweet.

Hack pulled Leti's legs to each side, gripping his thighs and rocking up. Leti's robes bunched, baring his full ass, and he gasped, then groaned into Hack's mouth, pushing his hips down, his dick hard against Hack's own cloth-covered one.

"Leti, my love, I need you." Hack moaned.

"Yes, but go slow, okay?"

"Anything you want." Hack twisted the two of them around so that he pressed on top of Leti. "Can I come inside you?"

Leti looked at him with swollen lips and dazed eyes and nodded. "I want that, Will. I want you inside me."

"Have you ever been with someone, Leti?"

Leti looked up from kissing his neck. "What's that matter? Just go slow."

"I haven't been with a man before, and you're my mate. I want this to be perfect."

"You've never been with a man? Aren't you attracted to men?"

"Yeah, I've been attracted to men before, but I just always seemed to gravitate to women. It was easier. You, though, you make me nervous. I want to get this right."

Leti giggled. "I make *you* nervous? Strangely, that makes me really happy since I'm the virgin here. It's okay though. We don't have to do anything we don't want to do. Let's just do what feels good right now, okay?"

"Sounds good." Hack brought his lips back to Leti's,

kissing him deeply. Leti wrapped his legs around Hack's hips and arched up into him, dick rubbing hard against Hack's stomach. Hack's own hard length settled against Leti's crease, sliding up and down with their movements. *Fuck,* he'd explode if he wasn't careful.

"Hack, can you move faster?" Leti asked. "Please?"

He moaned when Hack increased his pace and kissed him harder. Both men were panting, close to release from just a few touches. Then they were there. Leti cried out, arching up and shuddering, cum soaking the front of Hack's shirt. Hack followed close behind him, hot cum filling his pants, shudders racking through him. His body went limp, pressing Leti into the bed.

The two men stayed that way, wrapped up in each other for several moments.

"I'm sorry, Leti," Hack finally said. "I didn't mean to come so fast. I wanted to be inside you."

Leti laughed shakily, still short of breath. "That was perfect, Will. You were perfect. We'll get there when we get there. Don't rush, just enjoy."

Hack smiled down at him, then reluctantly rolled over into the pillows. A fierce hiss and bellow made him sit straight up. "What the fuck?"

A large, six-foot-long, one-foot-wide, scaled reptile slithered out from the stack of pillows, steam pouring from its nostrils and a puff of fire coming from its mouth.

"Princess Buttercup, you had better behave!" Leti leaned over and thumped the monster's nose. The reptile ducked its head and hummed deep in its chest.

"I know you're sorry, but you can't set my mate on fire. I kind of like him."

Hack watched in amazement as Princess crawled over to Leti and settled into his lap, curling around him and rubbing his head against Leti's forehead. His scales were different shades of red, varying from dark to light.

"How did he fit into that small carrier before?" Hack asked.

"Princess is a Fire Veil Dragon. He can actually shift sizes. When we travel, he stays about a foot long, but when he's home, he's usually anywhere from four to eight feet. I don't know for sure how big he can get, but he's never gotten above ten feet long, and three feet wide. I've had him twenty years, and he's my baby boy."

"Oh, gods." Hack could see it. Leti happily walking through the station with a fucking dragon, scaring every mercenary he came across. Were they even legal?

"You don't mind, do you?" Leti sounded uncertain. "He's my oldest pet, and he's really a sweetheart. He's just been through a lot today."

Hack melted. "Of course, I don't mind. He's your pet and you love him, so that means I love him too."

He leaned across and patted the dragon's back. Princess turned to look at him, yellow eyes glaring, and he hissed.

"Good boy," Hack grumbled.

Leti laughed. "He'll warm up to you. It took him a couple of weeks before he stopped hissing at Draif. Anyway, your crew's stolen all my pets. All I have left are Princess Buttercup, Wobble, and half my Druffles."

Hack laughed. "What?"

"You have Gravy, and Monty's adopted a reluctant Dru. This afternoon, Cordy took Biscuit and Juniper stole Pork Chop and Miss Speckles. Marmalade has always really belonged to Draif, but Selene took Fluffle. I don't think I'll be getting her back. Also, I'm giving half my Druffle collection to Ava. She loves them too much for me to say no. Finally, Beck told me that your pilot has fallen in love with Hector. He sits on the back of his chair as he flies the ship, and he's already made him a nest in his quarters."

"I'm sorry, baby," Hack said. "I guess I'll have to find you more pets to make up for it."

Leti smiled and kissed him. "Deal. How long until we're at Frost Veil?"

"Not too much longer. Coincidently, we're passing Fire Veil now." Hack gestured to the window where a tiny, red-and-orange planet dominated the view. "We'll be in Frost Veil's atmosphere in another three days. We'll have to wait on a permit to land once we arrive. There are four research facilities on planet, no cities or towns or spaceports. We have to have special permission to land at our client's private facility and that will take a little time."

"I've never been off Vextonar before. All of this is fascinating." Leti moved to the window, followed by Princess Buttercup. He hefted his dragon into his arms. "Look Princess, there's your home world, Fire Veil. Do you remember it?"

The dragon stared at the planet, then hissed.

"You *do* remember! It wasn't a nice place, was it? All those mean hunters chasing you."

Hack watched his mate talk to his dragon, smiling. This was his life now. Leti, Pepper, Draif, and his crew. His family.

7

"Then, Morgan said that I would outpace him in another week if I keep up my training."

Leti smiled, listening to his friend's excited voice. He brushed Wobble's thick hair while the llama ate cut-up carrots out of Draif's hands. Wobble's room was covered in straw, the air filter working overtime. Beck said he would adjust it to be more efficient once they stopped at Union Station. He needed more parts. He had already hung Wobble's toys up though. Wobble had a hanging container filled with apple slices to play with and several bells and rubber balls to swing around.

Beck had even adjusted the door so that the top and bottom opened separately. They left the top open, allowing Wobble to poke his head out and say hi to everyone as they passed in the hallway. Someone, Leti suspected Ava, had knitted him a bright red scarf that went well with his black and white fur.

"I'm glad you're settling in. Did you talk with

Dannol yet? He told Will that he'd love to start training you on piloting."

"Not yet. That's where I'm headed when we're done here." Draif patted Wobble's nose when he'd finished all the carrots, then wiped his slimy hand on a towel hanging over the door. "What are you going to do for the rest of the day? We'll be in Frost Veil in two more days, I think."

"I need to talk to Selene about training on some type of weapon," Leti said, tying Wobble's scarf neatly around his neck.

"What?" Draif yelled.

Leti frowned. "I just said that I need to talk to Selene about—"

Draif interrupted. "Yeah, I heard you. What I mean is: what the hell do you mean train on a weapon? Your father brought in every available tutor possible to try to tempt you with training, and you turned them all away. Now you *want* to train? What's going on?"

Leti moved from foot to foot, hesitant. "I don't want to say." It was Will's business, and he probably didn't want Leti spreading it around.

Draif pulled him over and into a tight hug. "Say or I'll never let you go. Going to the bathroom is going to get really awkward, really fast."

"Ugh, you are *so* annoying." Leti huffed, then sighed. "I can't tell you the details because they're not mine to give, but I want to be able to protect Will, just in case something bad happens."

Draif leaned back, incredulous. "You, the historian,

want to be able to protect your mate, the mercenary captain?"

"Yes." Leti nodded firmly. Why was that so hard to understand?

"Okay, then." Draif released him and stepped back. "You know that I'll guard him too, right? I get that he's important to you, just like your menagerie and Pepper. I'll protect all of them."

Leti cupped Draif's face. "Oh, Draify love. I know you're my protector, whether I want you to be or not, but sometimes a mate has to do what a mate has to do."

"What does that even mean?"

"It means I need to go talk to Selene, and you need to head over to the bridge."

Draif rolled his eyes. "Fine. Tell Selene to take it easy on you though. She's one tough lady."

Leti smiled and opened Wobble's door. "I don't need her to take it easy on me. I have a lot of catching up to do."

He left Draif to his own devices and headed toward the training room, passing one of the little cleaners sliding around the floors. Beck had put more out since the chickens were running all over the place. They weren't exactly potty-trained like the others. The cats had their litter boxes and the dogs and Pork Chop had a nice stretch of fake grass in the cargo area. Princess Buttercup used the toilet. Leti started giggling, remembering Will's face this morning when he opened the bathroom door to find Princess already using the facilities.

Leti sat down on one of the benches lining the wall.

Selene was in the middle of her own training, motions graceful and quick. Leti had never seen that type of fighting style before, but then again, fighting wasn't his thing. Fluffle stood watching her. When the cat saw Leti, he came over, winding between his feet before sitting in his lap with a purr.

Leti waited for Selene to finish, petting Fluffle. "Have you been a good cat for Selene? That's good. Yes, I miss you, but you've found your forever person and that's a fine thing."

Lucas, Morgan, Cordy, and Finn were doing their own training, paired off together. Alois came in, dressed in loose clothing, and was about to join them. He paused when he saw Leti, grinned, and headed his way. "How's it going?"

Leti smiled brightly, happiness filling every part of him. "Perfectly." He patted the seat next to him and Alois sat. "Thank you for your help. It's made things smoother and less awkward with my mate." He smiled slyly. "Now, we need to find you a mate."

Leti expected Alois to groan and deny any need to settle down, but instead, the Dedril sighed dreamily. "One can hope, Leti. One can hope."

"You want to settle down with one person? You seem very happy sharing the love."

"Do you know that the Dedril have mates as well? We find them through taste, usually a kiss." He leaned back in his seat. "So, I kiss a lot of men, but every time it's a disappointment. The man could be the most attractive, fascinating person, but it will still be a disappointment." He shrugged. "Don't get me wrong, I like sex, but one day, that kiss is going to happen, and I hope for it every day."

"Oh, Alois," Leti said. He reached over, hugging his friend. "I swear every time I talk to you, I like you more and more."

Alois hugged him back. "Good, because I like you too. You're very easy to talk to. Not that the crew are hard to get along with, but our group are all mercenaries. It's like there's a certain way we think we need to act, and it usually doesn't include talking about hopes and dreams. You and your menagerie have been good for us."

Selene sat on Leti's other side. "Why are you hugging? Did someone die?"

Leti sat back and turned to her. "No one died. Why would someone need to die for us to be hugging? Doesn't Dannol hug all the time? Will was grumbling about that last night."

Selene shrugged. "Dannol's a Havenite. Usually, they're overly affectionate, gentle, and far too perky."

Alois nodded. "This is very true." He looked Leti up and down, noting his own loose pants and baggy sweater covered in cacti. "What are you doing here, by the way? Not that you're not welcome, but this doesn't look like your scene."

"I was going to ask Selene to train me on a weapon."

Alois gaped, staring at him. Selene cocked her head, expression blank.

"Which weapon?" she asked.

"Wait now. Why do you need to know how to fight? Why do you *want* to know how to fight?" Alois started to get angry. "Is someone threatening you? Who is it? I'll take care of it."

"Why is everyone so surprised?" Leti groaned. "I just need to know how to protect Will, just in case something bad happens. For the love of chocolate squirrels, I'm not going to start doing missions!"

Alois grinned, brown eyes wide and soft. "Aww, that's so sweet. Leti's going to protect the captain."

"Which weapon?" Selene asked again. She could be waiting patiently, or she could be getting angry. Leti couldn't tell, damn it.

"I don't know. I always thought the kilij was interesting. The Old-Earth Ottoman Empire used them. One of my professors had one in his collection. Wouldn't that be great? I could wear a kaftan and a pair of salvar. I could call myself, Yusuf the Terrible."

Alois laughed so hard he fell out of his chair, then he just lay on the floor laughing. The other crewmembers couldn't resist coming over.

"What's going on?" Cordelia asked. "Why is this idiot rolling on the floor?"

"Leti is going to learn how to use a plasma phaser," Selene said. She got up and pulled Leti behind her. "Come on, Yusuf."

"Yusuf the Terrible. Oh gods." Alois laughed harder.

"What are you laughing at?" Lucas growled. "That sounds like a kickass name."

Hack leaned back in his seat in the conference room.

"Something seems strange about this request. Why hire a mercenary group to simply travel between planets and claim to expect no trouble? What do we know about Verion Morrick?"

Dru pulled up his profile, and it popped up in the center of the table. Morrick was a middle-aged human hybrid. He had Havenite, Wello, Vextonian, and Human blood in his ancestry, like many people in the galaxy.

"He has worked at the same research facility for the past twenty years," Dru said. "He's divorced, one kid aged twenty-two, both the ex and the kid live in a different system."

"Anything stand out?"

"He studied genetics and epidemiology at his university and has published over one hundred books and three hundred and sixty-two articles. That's a lot for a forty-two-year-old, even for a well-respected scientist. He is credited with creating over forty-six antidotes to viruses ranging from common to rare. Oh, and he developed the cure for soldi pox."

"That is a lot of accomplishments for a forty-two-year-old. What about the element?"

"Now, that is where it gets a little strange." The picture changed to feature a small, polished-bronze pyramid. Unfamiliar markings covered it. "The research center he works for didn't acquire anything even slightly resembling the element. Also, they show his current projects will have him on Frost Veil for the next five years, if not longer."

"Yet he's traveling to research this *element* on our station for the foreseeable future."

"Yeah, so is the center keeping it hush-hush, or did he privately acquire the element himself?"

"I don't know, but something just doesn't seem right here," Hack said. "What do we know about the element?"

"Absolutely nothing. This picture was sent to us by Morrick himself. Did the admiral say anything when you spoke with him?"

"No, but he was distracted."

"Oh, was he? Whatever could have distracted your father?"

"Shut it, Drusilla," Hack said, grinning. His smile faded as he stared at the simple artifact. "Something's not right."

"Does it make you nervous he studies infectious diseases? It makes me nervous." Dru shuddered.

Hack shrugged. "Maybe that's it. A lot of damage has been done with biological warfare. Whole species have disappeared."

"Well, we just have to give him a ride," Dru said. "What's the plan for pick-up?"

"Let's bring extra folks, just in case." He pulled up the layout of the space dock at the facility. "It should just be a matter of escorting him to the ship."

"Let's hope it stays simple, boss."

Hack pulled the vid-screen up and placed the call to his father. The admiral had given permission to Morrick, so maybe he knew something more. His father's broad, purple face popped up.

"You need something, son? I was about to call you myself." Hack's worry didn't lessen. The man looked a little frazzled, which was highly unusual.

"Why did you agree to have us escort Morrick and his element? Something seems off about the job, and we're trying to narrow it down."

"Oh, that. First, it was a job that brought you back to the station, which I wanted. Second, Orsla Manning requested it. Apparently, they're scholarly rivals and he asked her for a favor. She hasn't stopped crowing about it since I gave permission."

"So, no knowledge of what the element is," Dru asked.

"Not beyond the basics. It's a Post-Human Diaspora artifact from the Crellic System."

"Crellic System? I didn't think anything existed there anymore," Dru said, frowning.

His dad shrugged. His eyes were worried, and he kept scratching his ear. "Try Orsla. She was very excited about having it in her lab."

"Dad, are you alright? You mentioned that you were about to call me?"

Hack's dad froze, mid-ear scratch.

"Yes," he said eventually. "Dru, can you give us some privacy?"

She looked at Hack curiously, but got up, gathering her things. "No problem. Nice seeing you, Admiral."

He smiled fondly. "You too, Lady Fierce. Your husband is certainly looking forward to seeing you again next week."

"Gods, me too. I miss that man's ugly face," she said

and laughed as she left the room.

The admiral's smile fell away. "Son, I have some news, and I'm not sure how you're going to respond."

"That's not ominous or anything. Spit it out," Hack said, leaning back in his chair.

"The newest recruit did the Dead Ridge run on Burnished Outpost this morning."

Hack froze in his seat. There had only been three people picked up since he was found, two elder Burnished who had been close to death and one infant. She had been quickly adopted out to a Havenite family.

"They found a thirteen-year-old boy. We did the normal blood tests to check to see if he had family off planet." His father winced, reluctant to talk. "He's your half-brother."

"Half-brother?"

"He told us that his eldest brother was sacrificed, like him, and his mother remarried. He is the third oldest of his parents' seven children. He doesn't know you're alive. I wanted to check with you. What do you want me to do, son?"

"Why did they leave him?" Hack knew he would take care of him, but curiosity drove him. The thought of his mother making the choice to abandon another child crushed him.

Fasi sighed. "His mother just gave birth to the youngest and decided that seven children was one too many. He said of the three boys, he was the only one who couldn't call his fire." He looked sad. "Honestly, I think it has something to do with his rabbit."

"Rabbit?"

"He had a rabbit with him. It's fat and sassy while he is clearly malnourished. Hell, he even has a special brush he made for it."

"Pets aren't really a thing on Burnished Outpost. They're considered useless."

His dad's eyes softened and he smiled. "Sounds familiar, doesn't it?"

Hack sat back, horrified. "I was becoming just like them, wasn't I?"

"Your mother thinks you were overcompensating because you were afraid of losing your space with us. You know you'll always be our son, right? We love you."

Hack snorted. "I have never, not once, doubted that Fasi and Renee Juren love me. Mom is full of shit. It was probably just subconscious bullshit."

Laughter boomed through the vid-screen. "Fair enough. What do you want me to do about the boy? We can find him a good home or…"

"He'll stay with Leti and me of course. Gods, Leti would kick my ass if I turned my own brother away," Hack said. He smiled sheepishly before admitting, "I would kick my own ass too."

Fasi smiled. "That was what I'd hoped you'd say. To be honest, if you couldn't take him, Renee and I would have. We've already made up your old room for him. Fuck, now we need to upgrade your rooms again. We moved all your shit to a two-bedroom. Now, you'll need a three-bedroom."

Hack laughed. "Make sure there's room for Wobble the llama and the fucking dragon."

"Llama? Wait, did you say dragon?"

"Princess Buttercup is a Fire Veil dragon," Hack said. "That uses the toilet."

"Oh my."

Hack grinned, then sighed softly, strangely calm. "What's his name, Dad?"

"Moses Hackett. I changed his last name on his records already to match yours. Calls himself Mo."

"Thanks, dad."

"No problem, son. Love you."

Hack entered his room, tired and soul sore. Gravy followed behind him and quickly found his food bowl. Leti was stretched out on the bed, spooning Princess Buttercup. The two were fast asleep. Hack smiled and closed the door. He was ready for a nap himself.

A WET, hot mouth woke Hack up from his nap. Leti had Hack's pants pulled down and his lips wrapped around Hack's cock. Hack moaned, arched his back, and ran his fingers through Leti's hair.

Leti tried to take more of him down his throat, but gagged a bit, pulling back and sucking Hack's tip. It didn't take long and Hack was groaning and shooting into his mouth.

Leti pulled off his spent cock and licked his lips. "That was much more fun than I thought it would be when Draif mentioned it."

Hack lifted his head from his pillow, looking at his mate's dancing green eyes. "Draif told you to give me a blow job?"

"No, he just mentioned what it was a few years ago. Sounded awkward and disgusting. That was pure delicious though."

"Anytime you want to do that again, baby, you just let me know," Hack said, pulling his mate up and out of the bed. He fastened his pants. "Did Juniper drop off dinner tonight?"

"Nope. Beck's bringing it when he leaves Pepper with us."

Hack's pleasant buzz started to fade. "That reminds me. We need to talk."

Leti's smile disappeared. "I haven't had a relationship before, but even I know that's not a good phrase. Did I do something wrong? Was the blow job not good? I can get better. I promise." His panic had reached his eyes and his lips trembled. He was close to tears. "I can try to lose some weight. I just really like food."

"No, baby," Hack said quickly, pulling his mate into his arms. "You are absolutely amazing. I loved the blow job, and you are perfect just the way you are. You never have to worry about me trying to end our relationship. You're utterly necessary, like air."

Leti shuddered and released his breath. "Sorry about that. I hadn't realized I felt so... I don't know what to call it. Needy? Vulnerable?"

"It's doesn't feel like it, but we've only known one another a couple of days. Our relationship is forged steel, I know it is, but we haven't tested it yet, so it feels fragile, breakable," Hack said. "Baby, it's not though. Nothing short of death would make me leave you."

Leti rubbed his face against Hack's chest. "What did you need to talk about?"

Hack led him to a couple of chairs, and they sat. "My dad called today. You remember when I told you Charybdis Station has new recruits running patrols along Dead Ridge on Burnished Outpost?"

"Yeah," Leti said slowly. His eyes widened. "Oh gods, did they find someone? Are they alright? Do they need somewhere to stay? They can stay with us. They're your people, and if they were abandoned too, then they need us!"

Hack smiled, pulling Leti into his lap.

"Gods, I love you." He kissed the top of Leti's head. "They found my half-brother. He's thirteen and he has a pet rabbit."

"Your brother? A rabbit? I love rabbits. What's his name?"

"My brother or the rabbit?" His mate was so damn adorable.

"Both!"

Hack laughed. "My brother's name is Mo, and I don't know his rabbit's name. You don't mind if he lives with us?"

"Of course not! I came with Pepper and you come with Mo. It's perfect."

Princess Buttercup crawled out from under the bed, quickly moving onto Leti's lap. He laid his head on Hack's other shoulder and hissed. "You also come with a dragon and a llama. Princess won't eat Mo's rabbit, will he?"

"No," Leti giggled. "Princess is a vegetarian."

8

SILVERLIGHT SYSTEM, PLANET FROST VEIL

After a night of heavy sleep cuddled next to his mate, Leti sat in a chair in Draif's room, petting Marmalade and watching his friend dig through his closet, searching for something. The room was now as fully furnished as Leti and Will's. Each member of the crew, including Will, had gifted something of their own to Draif. Dru had already volunteered her painting skills again once Draif decided on a color.

Leti was happy that Draif had his own personal space for the first time in his life. He had his own belongings and was fast on his way to forging his own future. It was the first time Leti had ever seen Draif nervous though.

"What's wrong with the body armor you're wearing? Isn't that the standard for a mission?" Leti asked.

"Yes, but I wanted to bring my favorite phasers too and I can't find them."

"Do you have your new knives?"

"Yeah, they're hidden in my boots." He jumped up, waving a phaser in each hand. "Found them!"

Leti laughed. "Do you like the rifle Will gave you?"

"It's great, but I'm still attached to my phasers. Remember when you gave them to me?"

"Yes, I do. I never expected to see someone so happy from being gifted a weapon."

Draif plopped down in the chair across from Leti. "Weapons do make me happy." He watched Leti carefully. "How are you doing? We've only been here a few days, but a lot has happened."

Leti grinned, full of happiness. "I'm wonderful. I woke up in my mate's arms, then had a wonderful breakfast. I visited with Wobble, who is doing very well, then I held and fed Pepper completely by myself. Now, I'm watching my best friend get ready for his very first mission."

Draif laughed, shaking his head. "I never thought I'd see you so happy. You never seemed interested in any of the men or women your mother sent your way. Usually, you just ignored them and spent time with me or your pets. I'm glad you found someone." His expression grew serious. "Love has its own troubles too, Leti. The amount you care for another person is the same amount that they can hurt you."

Leti sent his friend a sympathetic look. "I know what that bastard did to you. You're right, of course." He looked away. "I don't want to be cautious though. I want to jump in all the way and risk everything. I can't seem to help myself."

Draif was quiet for a minute. "I don't think that's a bad thing. As much as I regret how it ended for me, when I had him, when I thought he was mine, it was beyond beautiful. I can't begrudge you that, and gods, I hope your chance doesn't end. Captain Will Hackett is not Beldon Cortez though. He is a much better man."

Levi smiled softly, aware of how much it cost Draif to say the man's name. "He *is* a much better man, and I know that you'll find someone too. Someone who will see the wonder you are and not a past you were born into."

Draif seemed to shake himself, visibly putting the past behind him. "I really like it here, Leti, but we need to make a Plan B in case things go south. I'm setting aside any pay I get, but we need to think ahead, just in case."

"Would it make you feel more settled?"

"Yes, but more importantly, you'd be more protected."

Leti dug around in his pocket and pulled out two separate credit chips. He handed them both to Draif. "I split all that I saved into two, unassigned credit chips. One for you and one for me. Anyone who has possession of them can cash them. Take them and invest them. I know you paid a lot more attention to the financial lessons that Father made me sit through, so you have the better chance of being successful."

"Leti, are you sure? That's a lot of money," Draif said. "What if I mess up?"

Leti shrugged. "Then you mess up. Honestly, I don't

need a Plan B. I'm where I belong, with Will, but I think it'll make you feel better."

Draif looked determined. "I'll do my best. Since I got my hands on a little tech, I've been researching some stocks. I have an idea."

Leti laughed. "Of course, you do. What's the plan for the morning? Shouldn't we have the permit to land soon?"

"Yeah. The captain, Selene, Alois, Lucas, Cordelia, and I are going to meet with the client and escort him to the ship. It seems excessive, but the captain said something felt off. I don't know."

"Well, please be careful. I love you and don't know what I would do without you."

Draif stood and pulled Leti into a hug. "I'll be careful. I'll keep an eye on your man too. Can't have you crying if he gets hurt."

Leti hugged him tightly. "You both better come back."

HACK WAS WAITING BACK in their room when Leti returned from visiting Draif. He had an early dinner laid out on the table and food and water already in Gravy and Princess Buttercup's bowls. Gravy was asleep in his bed, snoring softly, and Princess was stuffing his face.

Hack pulled out Leti's chair, then sat across from him, but he looked a little distracted.

"What's wrong?" Leti asked.

Hack shrugged, uncertain. "I don't know. I just have a feeling something's going to go wrong tomorrow." He stopped talking and looked horrified. "Oh gods, I shouldn't have said that to you. You're probably already nervous about Draif's first mission."

Leti laughed. "I certainly don't want anything to go wrong tomorrow, but I know this is what you do, what Draif is going to be doing. Yes, I'm nervous, but I know that I'm here with you now, and I'm going to be here when you all get back." He grabbed Hack's hand. "We'll figure it out. I can't say I'll ever not worry about you, but I don't think that would be a good thing."

"No," Hack agreed. "My mom and dad never seemed nervous when one of them went on a mission, but they always tried to be there when the other returned. I guess I never thought of it as a way of coping, just happenstance. They are both mercenaries though."

"Well, I'm a historian, which means I can work on whichever ship you're on. I may not fully understand what you go through on a day-to-day basis like your parents do, but I will be right here waiting on you."

Hack grinned and shoveled food into his mouth. "Hurry up and eat. I want to play. Beck's bringing Pepper by in a few hours."

"I see what's important to you." Leti huffed but ate faster, eager to *play* himself. In a matter of minutes, the two men had empty plates and were stretched out on the bed, kissing.

Leti's hands wanted more skin today. He had gotten to pet his mate this morning, but he wanted more. He unbuttoned Hack's shirt and slid it off his shoulders. His lips traced a trail to Hack's little, erect nipples, stopping to kiss each one. He continued down his chest to his abdomen, then his cloth-covered cock. Leti placed an open-mouthed kiss to his dick, Hack's moans echoing across the room.

"Fuck, Leti," he said, running his hands through Leti's hair and pulling his head up, lips caressing his again. "I want to come inside you tonight. Let's save your mouth for later."

Leti sat up, crawling atop his mate. "Sounds good to me."

He pulled off his sweater, tossing it across the room, and rocked his hips against Hack's hard length. He never thought he'd be so uninhibited, but Hack loved him and his body, even his little belly.

Hack grabbed Leti's hips and rolled him beneath him. He unbuttoned Leti's pants and pulled them off, along with his underwear, tossing them next to his sweater.

Then his mouth was on Leti's cock.

"Oh gods," Leti gasped. "Oh gods, don't stop."

Hack smiled around his dick and sucked him deep. Leti arched his hips, moaning.

Hack cupped Leti's ass, running his fingers along his crease. He circled Leti's hole with a finger, feeling Leti's slick. He pulled back and off Leti. "Baby, do you have any Wello blood in your genes?"

Leti glared down at him, trying to put Hack's mouth back to where he wanted it—on his dick. "You want to talk about genetics right now?"

Hack laughed, and kissed the tip of Leti's dick. "You feel slick is all. If you have Wello blood, I might get you pregnant. That's kind of important."

"Ugh, yes, I'm a breeding male," Leti groaned. "Now, put your mouth back on my dick!"

"Yes, sir," Hack said, grinning. He returned to work, and he pushed a finger through the ring of nerves, stretching his mate's hole.

Leti grinned and rocked his hips, uncertain which direction to go. Hack's mouth felt so good, but so did his finger. *Oh gods.* Hack added another one.

When Hack slowly added a third, Leti thought he would explode.

"Hack, please," he whined. "Please."

Hack sat up, mouth leaving Leti's cock with a wet pop. He unbuttoned his own pants and stroked his dick, his gaze intense and hot. He reached between Leti's legs, gathering up his slick and rubbed it all over his own cock.

He pulled Leti's legs up, spreading them wide, and positioned himself at Leti's entrance. With a gentle shove and a little rocking, he was soon seated inside Leti, filling him completely.

Hack buried his face against Leti's neck and set a slow pace, sliding in and out of his mate's body. Leti wrapped his arms around Hack's neck and moved with him, arousal blinding him, consuming him.

A few minutes later, he was there, spraying his cum onto Hack's stomach and yelling. Hack's speed picked up and he was soon pounding into him, balls slapping against his ass.

"Leti…" He groaned, releasing into him, filling him with his hot seed.

Leti breathed hard, clutching his mate to him. "Hack," he said, voice shaky, unable to say what he was feeling. He had never been so intimate with someone, so vulnerable.

"Mate," Hack said, rubbing his face against Leti's. "I love you, Leti."

"Love you too," he finally managed to get out.

LATER THAT NIGHT, Leti held Pepper close and rocked her, hoping she'd go back to sleep. Will was finally fast asleep in the bed. He was really worried about tomorrow and had tossed and turned for a while. Leti had yet to fall asleep himself when he'd heard Pepper's little whimpers, building up to a cry. He had managed to change, feed, and burp Pepper without waking Hack, but now she wouldn't go back to sleep.

He sat in the rocker in the corner of Pepper's little section of the room. How Beck had managed to make a rocking chair out of old junk parts, Leti didn't know. It was damn comfortable too. The man was a genius. He had built this rocker and the baby's bassinet in a day. Leti had expected jagged edges when Beck first mentioned his projects, but everything was rounded, smooth, and warm. They were works of art, as original as their gentle creator. Ava had provided a perfectly sized pillow to act as a temporary mattress and Pepper was all set.

Leti tucked his favorite soft, crocheted blanket around Pepper and stared into her big, green eyes. He never thought he'd want babies, but here he was. Now that he saw her, smelled her, heard her, he completely and irrevocably loved her. As she got bigger, she'd move into her own room, but until then, Leti was glad to have her close. He was getting used to holding a baby, but he didn't think his nervousness would ever go away. She was so tiny, and right now, so unhappy.

He had to get her to sleep, but he didn't know any lullabies. His mother certainly had never sung any. He did know ancient Old-Earth poets though. He closed his eyes, thinking of his favorite, an ancient Greek woman named Sappho.

"He's more than a hero, he's a god in my eyes. The man who's allowed to sit at your side," Leti sang in a soft, sweet voice, making up his own melody to fit his favorite poem. Pepper stopped whimpering and stared at him, green eyes luminous and wide. "He listens closely to the sweetness of your voice, the enticing laughter that makes my own heart beat fast."

Leti rocked Pepper gently, seeing her eyes start to flutter.

"If I meet you, I can't speak. My tongue's broken, and fire runs over my skin. I can't see, just hear my own heartbeat." His voice deepened. "I sweat and tremble, turning paler than dry grass."

He set a sleeping Pepper back in her beautiful bed.

"At such times death isn't far from me," he finished. He leaned down and kissed her, then turned around, still humming, and headed for bed and his mate's arms.

9

Hack surveyed the room as they waited for the scientist to show up. The management at the facility had been slow to accept any calls and were reluctant to agree to let Morrick off planet. He was a freeman, and employees of all the research facilities made trips off Frost Veil to visit family since they weren't allowed to live on planet. It was highly suspicious.

Then, they'd suddenly capitulated. After arguing for close to eight hours, they'd decided that the Blue Solace could land, no problem and sorry for the inconvenience. The only thing they wouldn't allow was a shuttle. The crew forced to walk the mile from the small space dock.

After getting the permit and landing, the six mercenaries had quickly headed to Facility B194A. The planet was basically one big ball of ice and snow, so the walk hadn't been pleasant. Hack thought his balls might have frozen off. He couldn't really be sure because of the numbness.

At least the waiting room was warm, but Morrick was supposed to have met them ten minutes ago. Hack did not like this.

"This room is not secure," Selene said. "There are three entrances and no security."

"Doesn't seem too smart for an important facility, right?" Cordelia looked around the large grey room. There was a security station—it just wasn't currently occupied. A cooling cup of coffee sat on the desk.

"This doesn't feel right, Captain," Alois said, spinning around the empty room.

One entrance suddenly opened and Verion Morrick came in at a run. "We have to go now!" he said. He had a bag slung over his shoulder and blood on his shirt. Panic lit his eyes as he darted toward the exit. Alois, Cordelia, Lucas, and Draif instantly surrounded him, running in formation as they left the building, going back to the snowy, barren landscape.

"A Concord ship landed half a mile away five minutes ago," Morrick puffed out as he ran.

"The Concord? Gods damn it!" Hack growled and took point, Selene bringing up the rear. "Let's get gone fast." The Concords were another group of mercenaries, but they took jobs that no one with even a smidgen of honor or decency would take. They were known for their cruelty and intolerance of non-human species.

"They can't get either me or the element," Morrick panted. "People will die, billions and billions of people."

"They won't get you," Hack said. "Now, shut up and move." The group traveled quickly, but Morrick was a scientist, not a mercenary, so Hack knew they couldn't keep up the current pace.

"Dannol, you read?" Hack called the ship, breath puffing out in the cold.

"What do you need, Cap?"

"We have a Concord ship about half a mile from our meeting point. Do you read anyone running to intercept us?"

"Wait a sec… I can't read anything, Captain. This planet messes with the ship's instruments every time we land. I'll do it old school."

Morrick was starting to slow down, drawing in air and panting. Alois picked him up and tossed him over his shoulder, never pausing. "Got him, Captain."

"Good job, keep moving everyone."

"Captain," Dannol's voice came through the comm. "I see a shuttle headed your way. They are about a quarter mile away and closing fast."

"Fuck."

"Dru and the others are headed your way with our shuttle. Find cover, fast. There are rocks right ahead."

Hack looked around. The grouping of icy rocks was just a little ways in front of them. "Shields up, people, we have incoming. Get behind those rocks, now!"

Each crew member activated their shields, except Alois. He placed his small, circular shield button on Morrick before activating it, the light plasma deflector covering the scientist from head to toe.

They didn't make it to the rocks in time. The

Concord shuttle began firing long before it came within range of their own weapons. The bombarding plasma bolts weren't accurate, but there was enough of it. Lucas fell, hit in the leg, shield shattered. Draif stopped to pick him up, throwing the much larger man over his shoulder with ease.

Alois got hit next, dropping to the ground and not moving. Morrick rolled from his hold, got up, and continued toward the rocks.

"Selene, get them to those rocks," Hack yelled. He turned to face the shuttle, standing over Alois. Plasma bolts pelted his shield, but it held for now. His markings began to glow with a blinding gold light. He called for his fire, desperate. Things had gone wrong so fast.

His eyes lit up from within, burning brightly. He pulled more deeply than he ever had before. As the shuttle pulled into range, Hack sent every bit of molten heat he could toward it. A large, golden burst of heat tunneled from him and into the metal, blasting a large hole in the front of the shuttle. It went down, sliding through snow and ice. Hack picked up Alois and ran as the shuttle slid closer, his boots crunching in the snow. He could feel exhaustion pulling at him, a deep cold seeping into his bones.

The Concord mercenaries burst from the shuttle, at least sixteen. They pulled weapons and ran toward Hack's group, firing. Hack's leg buckled, shot, as his shield finally gave. He fell, dropping an unconscious Alois. He rolled, lying over his crewman, and fired at the approaching group.

Selene threw a plasma grenade from behind her rock, hitting several of the Concord. Draif darted out, firing from his twin plasma phasers, hitting each target dead on, shots accurate enough to pierce shields. The small man moved toward Hack, Cordelia and Lucas covering him from the rocks.

"Get Alois, Draif. I'll follow."

"Yes, sir." As Draif ducked to pick up Alois, Hack's shuttle arrived, firing at the remaining Concord, cutting them down.

Hack breathed a sigh of relief and saw that Draif had gotten Alois back to the rocks. Finn landed the shuttle and opened the back hatch.

Hack's relief was short-lived.

"Captain, you have another shuttle coming up," Dannol said through the comm.

The hum of the shuttle approaching reached Hack's ears.

"Fuck. Load up and get out," Hack yelled, dragging himself to his feet. "Another one's coming."

The speeding shuttle dived toward Hack's group at the rocks, firing at Dru's shuttle, landing between it and the rocks, effectively blocking their escape. Concord mercenaries poured out of the back, firing.

Selene stood and drew her blades. She ran through the crowd of mercenaries, her movements graceful and efficient, leaving dead men behind her.

Cordelia and Draif stood in front of Morrick and Alois, firing at the approaching mercenaries. The scientist lay over Alois, his shield taking the occasional hit as he protected the unconscious man. Lucas leaned against the rocks and tossed grenades toward the Concord shuttle. It was too far away to directly hit, but the mercenaries still pouring out of it were close enough.

Hack stumbled but reached the fight, his phaser firing in one hand and molten heat pouring from the other. He couldn't pull much of his fire now, but it was enough to burn a man to a crisp, shielded or not.

Dru and Morgan came from around the enemy shuttle, one at each side. They whooped loudly as they joined the battle, and the attention of the Concord switched to them. Morgan cut a path through the mercenaries, vibro-blades swirling around him. He headed for Draif's group. Dru laughed like a crazy person, Monty clinging to her head, and fired shot after shot, plasma bolts hitting their marks.

Taking advantage of the distraction, Beck darted around the Concord ship and barreled through the battle, reaching Morrick and Alois. He picked both men up and slung one over each shoulder. Then the massive Grell quickly darted back through the crowds to their shuttle.

With the scientist missing and facing fire from both sides, the Concord mercenaries lost form and chaos took over. Selene cut down enemy mercs as they turned to run toward the ship, blades slicing deep.

"Lucas," Draif yelled, turning toward the man and firing at the mercenaries dragging him away. Hack limped behind him, diverting the blade aimed for Draif's head with his phaser, then setting the attacker on fire.

Draif turned, facing two more opponents and quickly finished them off. Before long, the Concord shuttle was pulling back into the sky, shooting off to the main ship.

"Fuck, roll count," Hack said. The battle had taken less than five minutes, but his crew looked rough. Dead bodies were piled around the grouping of rocks with more scattered back the way they had come. Draif leaned against him, pulling Hack's arm around him and helping him limp toward the shuttle.

"Good," Dru and Selene said at once.

"Good, shot to the arm," Cordelia said, breathing hard and walking slowly toward the shuttle.

"Good, minor cuts and one deep wound in the thigh," Morgan said, putting Hack's other arm around his shoulders.

"Finn, Morrick, and me are good. Finn's ready to fly us to the ship and we need to get Alois to Doc, fast," Beck said from the shuttle, making room for Hack to sit on the bench inside.

"They took Lucas," Draif said angrily. "I couldn't get to him in time." Draif looked devastated. "We need to get him back."

"Oh, we will," Hack said, his face grim. He knew his eyes were glowing with his fire. "We will."

<hr>

As the shuttle slowly approached the dock, stuttering and grinding from the hits it had taken, Hack noticed the doors to the dock were shattered, knocked wide open from within. "What happened here?"

"The fuckers wouldn't open the doors to let our shuttle out," Beck said, growling with anger. "We told them you all were being attacked and they just smiled."

"Didn't sit well with us, so we opened them ourselves," Finn said.

"Why wouldn't they let you through though?" Cordelia asked. She clutched her arm, blood seeping through slowly.

"They knew the Concords were coming," Morrick said. His face was pale, eyes sunken. He looked far older than his forty-two years. "My colleagues, people I thought were good, I thought were fighting to save lives…" He closed his eyes, a tear trailing down one cheek. "The management called the Concords in. Together, they all work for someone. I don't know who, but I know what they want." He sat beside Alois and reached for his hand.

"Why didn't you warn us? Did you just discover this?" Hack didn't think the man would purposely put his own life in danger, but nothing about this situation made a lot of sense.

"I discovered a few concerning things about the element last week and talked to my bosses. They acted troubled and seemed happy I was taking the artifact to Charybdis Station to do further studies. As much as our facility has and can do, they don't have Orsla Manning. Between the two of us, we can figure this thing out." Morrick paused, looking away from Alois, eyes meeting Hack's. "I'm sorry your man was hurt and the other taken. If I could have, I would have warned you. A few days ago, right after I spoke with them, management suddenly cut off my communication to the outside world and locked me in my rooms. My assistant tried to help me, and they killed her, right in front of me."

"*Gods*. What the fuck is going on?" Dru said.

"Before she was murdered, Nina was able to do two things. First, she smuggled the element and my notes to her cousin on Union Station. Second, she hacked my bosses' computers. I read through their communications with the Concords. I don't know who they work for, but I know that they plan to use the element to destroy planets. I think they're aiming for the Boral System first, but I don't know why or what they could possibly gain. The destruction could potentially wipe out whole species."

"We'll talk more on the ship," Hack said. The shuttle landed and Nettle and Leti met them at the hatch with a gurney. Alois was quickly loaded and carried to the medical bay. Morrick followed behind them, intent on helping the wounded.

"I expect every last one of you to show in my med bay within the hour, wounded or not," Nettle called back over his shoulder as he rushed out.

Leti was in Hack's arms within seconds, face burrowing into him. Gravy and Princess Buttercup sat beside them, the large dog whining with concern and the dragon looking constipated. Hack hugged his mate tightly, ignoring the throbbing in his leg.

Various pets trailed in, greeting their new

companions and checking to make sure they were alright. Selene nodded to Fluffle and pushed Cordelia toward the med bay. Cordelia sniffled into Biscuit's fur, arm clearly causing her pain.

Leti pulled a passing Draif into their hug. "You guys alright?"

"Your man got shot, but I'm okay," Draif answered.

"What happened to Alois? Where's Lucas?" Leti stepped away from Hack and pulled his mate's arm around his shoulders. "Off to the med bay for you, love."

"Dannol," Hack said as Draif filled Leti in on what had happened.

"Yes, Cap?" Dannol's voice came through his comm.

"Let's get the fuck off this planet. We have a ship to hunt down."

10

_L_eti sat at Alois's bedside with Varion Morrick. Pepper was strapped to his chest, sleeping peacefully. Alois was still unconscious. Nettle said that he'd been shot close to his heart, and the scales on his chest were scorched away. Nettle had finished the surgery needed, but he didn't know if Alois would make it. He had lost a lot of blood.

Nettle moved around the room quickly, tending to the less serious injuries of the rest of the crew. Ava followed in his wake, aiding him when she could. Cordelia's wounds were the worst, the arm wound just one of many. She had lost more blood then they originally thought, and she was currently sedated for the pain. Nettle had given in and let Biscuit cuddle against her side.

Once Hack was quickly patched up, he dropped a kiss on Leti's head and limped off to the bridge with Gravy, Dru, Selene, and Draif. They had plotting to do and a ship to trail after. They were determined to get

Lucas back as quickly as possible. The Concords were known for their love of torture.

Leti held Alois's hand. "I just met him a few days ago, but he's already my friend. We can't lose him. He needs to kiss his mate, fall in love."

Morrick sighed and patted Leti's shoulder. "I hope you don't lose him. Life has a way of surprising a person with sudden turns, twisting and looping to Hell and back. I hope this is just a short deviation for him, but what will be, will be."

"I always hated that saying," Leti said. "I want to make things better, not passively accept the bad things."

Morrick smiled sadly. "I used to feel that same way. Then, about five years ago, I ran into a problem that I couldn't fix. I couldn't control it. Every choice I made up to that point had led to and created that problem, and suddenly, I was out of chances and redos. It threw me for a loop, that's for sure. Made me see life a little differently. Now, I do think we need to work on making things happen the way they ought to, but when there's something that we can't control? That we can't change? There's no sense in ruining our future by dwelling on it." He laughed softly. "That conversation got a lot more philosophical than I was expecting, and I do realize advice is easy to give but hard to take. I don't mean to sound patronizing."

"I get you, don't worry. You're probably right. It just hurts to think that Alois may never get the future he deserves." Leti looked the scientist over. He stood out for being average. He was average in height, about five foot eight, average in weight, around one hundred and fifty pounds, and average in looks, brown hair and eyes. The only thing not average was his obvious misery. "You look a little rough. Are you alright?"

Morrick smiled sadly. "I'm much better off than Alois here."

"That didn't answer my question."

"I'm not wounded. Your crew kept me safe."

"That still doesn't answer my question," Leti said persistently. The man's eyes were damn sad. "Remember what you just told me?"

Morrick grimaced. "I told you advice was easy to give and hard to take." He sighed. "I worked on Frost Veil at that research facility for twenty years. I lost my wife and son to my work, convinced that the good I was doing would more than make up for it. That I could connect with them, win them back, later." He slumped in his seat. "Now, I find out that the people I respected—my own supervisors—are plotting to kill billions of people, merely for not being human enough."

"I'm so sorry, Verion," Leti said. "It still amazes me to see how much others can hate."

"That's true. I thought my colleagues would at least be surprised, but when I confronted them, they just laughed. They don't care about other species. The callousness of it!" Morrick sat up. "Nina did though. She cared and she died for it."

"She was your assistant, right?"

"Yes," he answered. "So damn smart. There was so much potential in her. She got the element out of there, sent it to her cousin. So smart. She reminded me of..." Morrick trailed off.

"Of who?"

"My son, Wyatt." Morrick smiled softly, love lighting him from within, his face truly beautiful with its influence. "He's a medical doctor, traveling to poverty-stricken worlds to help people. He's not me; he doesn't stay in his lab, researching, researching, researching. He's out there, directly making a difference, and oh gods, is that boy bright. He made the best grades in school and university, but he's more than smart. He's kind, compassionate. He is so amazing and so damn stubborn. He can do anything he sets his mind to, that's for sure."

"He sounds wonderful. Do you get to see him often? You can call him, if you'd like."

Morrick's happiness drained away, face dull and empty. "He doesn't want to see me. When he was born, I was at work, and I think I stayed there until his mother divorced me. I hardly went home and barely spoke to him. He was seven when they left." He looked away from Leti, shame lighting up his cheeks. "I didn't talk to him again until he was sixteen. I never had time. I never *made* time. I told myself that I was making the world safer for him. Gods, I love him. By the time I realized what a complete idiot I was, it was too late. He refused to speak to me. Told me that he didn't have a father." Tears fell from Morrick's eyes. "I can't possibly blame him for it, but I will keep him safe. I will not let the artifact or my knowledge fall into the wrong hands."

Leti reached over and pulled the older man into a hug. "I'm sorry, Verion. I don't know how to make this better. Perhaps you should call him? It's been a few years, right? He may have changed his mind."

Morrick grimaced. "I doubt it. Even if he has, I don't need to draw attention to him. As it is, only Nina knew I gave a damn about him. I brought all the letters I wrote him through the years with me. Gods know, I never had the nerve to send them to him."

"You should give him another chance. If he's as kind as you say…"

"He is and you're right; he would probably forgive me." He looked away. "I don't deserve it."

***

HACK WATCHED the ship flying ahead of them. It was a battle cruiser and, he hated to say it, outmatched his own Blue Solace. Gravy stood on two legs, braced against the window, watching the ship and growling.

"You're sure they can't see us?" Draif's voice was suspicious.

"Yes, I created this stealth generator myself," Beck replied. "It gives us natural camouflage in case they look out a window, but it also prevents their sensors from picking up our presence. I haven't figured out how to make us invisible yet." He pouted from his chair, tail twitching in irritation.

"That's amazing," Draif said and Beck preened. Hack's engineer truly was a genius.

"How we doing this, boss?" Dru was eager to get

Lucas back. Fuck, Hack was too. He couldn't stand the idea of any of them hurt, but kidnapped, likely tortured? *Hell no.*

"Selene? I'm thinking a shuttle with a small team to infiltrate. What do you think?"

Selene studied the ship ahead of them, face expressionless. "Beck, are there any weaknesses to this model? Some way we can get in without them noticing?"

"Hmm, if we were in an atmosphere it wouldn't be a problem, but in space…" he mused. "There's a place where their landing gear comes out when they dock. It pressurizes when closed. It's close to the normal placement of cells on this model too. It's a two-man job though. No more than that would fit in the landing gear room along with Lucas and the equipment needed. The team can jump out our space lock, then drift on over to the ship, force the opening, get in, shut it back up, then go rescue Lucas."

"That sounds easy," Dru said sarcastically. "What's to stop the incredible speeds the ships are moving at from pulverizing us?"

"Our suits are a little special," Beck said, smiling smugly.

"Have you been tweaking with things again without my permission?" Hack didn't really mind, but he liked to tease the man since he got so excited about new engineering projects.

"Maybe," Beck said and shrugged. "Someone, and I'm not saying it was me, might have made them stable enough to wear outside a moving ship for a short period of time."

"Why would you think we needed that?" Dru seemed genuinely curious.

"Why wouldn't we?" Beck said with a shrug.

"I'm going," Draif said.

"Not happening, kid," Dru argued. "Selene and I will go."

Hack sighed. Dru was not going to like this. "Draif and Beck will go. End of discussion."

"What the fuck? *No!* He's just a kid. You can't ask him to do this."

"I *want* to do this," Draif said. "I *need* to do this. I didn't get to him in time."

Dru turned to Hack in disbelief. "So, you're just going to let him run off on guilt-ridden rescue trips? What about Beck? He's our engineer. He dies, our ship falls apart."

"You think I *want* to send anyone but myself?" Hack asked angrily. "Beck is going because he knows ships. He can get the shit done that we *need* done. Draif is going because he's the smallest and will take up less room in that tiny docking space. That's it." Hack turned to Draif. "As for you, *no one* got to Lucas in time. It's not on you. It's not on any of us. It's on those sick fucks in that ship. You get caught up in guilt over everything that happens and you will die fast and needlessly." His tone softened. "I feel it every time anything happens to my crew. I'm the captain. I should protect everyone."

"That's bullshit. You can't be everywhere at once," Draif said.

"Exactly. I can't and *you* can't. Being a soldier means you're putting yourself in danger. Lucas knows that. Doesn't mean we leave him behind. It just means we don't drown ourselves in guilt. We focus on getting him back."

"Okay," Draif said, face determined. "Let's do this."

"You said soldier, not mercenary," Selene said.

Hack blushed. "Yeah, you know what I mean."

"Hmm," she said.

"I'm surprised, Captain," Beck said. "You never miss a rescue mission. I remember when Cordelia got nabbed by those slavers on Union Station. You wouldn't let Dru go then either."

Hack smiled sheepishly. "Well, we won't be sitting on our thumbs here."

Dru grinned. "What are we doing?"

"Selene and I will be placing lovely bombs along the sides of the ship."

"Where'd they come from," Beck asked.

"She cooked them up a couple of weeks ago," Hack answered.

"We had some defunct grenades and pulse cannons. Waste not, want not," Selene said.

"So, what the fuck am I doing?" Dru was pissed off. She always did like to be involved.

"You'll be running the missions, shithead," Hack answered. "Someone has to make sure our asses get pulled back to the ship."

He turned to Dannol. "You okay to fly us as close to the ship as you can get? You'll have to clamp onto the ship and match their speed perfectly while we do this."

"I got this, Cap," Dannol said. "Just make sure to plant a couple of bombs for me. I hate always having to stay with the ship."

Dru put a hand on Draif's shoulder. "Come on, kid. I'll help you suit up. Beck, you're going to get your junk, right?"

"I'll gather it now." The Grell clapped his hands and jumped excitedly before running out of the room. *Maybe I should let him off the ship more often,* Hack thought.

"Wait, Draif, we better go say bye to Leti first. If he looks out a window and sees us, he'll probably be pissed," Hack said.

"Yeah, I can already see him fussing at us through the window."

Dru smiled sweetly. "Come along, gentlemen. Let's go tell Leti that the two men he loves the most are about to risk their fool necks."

She waltzed off the bridge as Gravy whined.

"Uh oh," Draif said, running out the door. By the time Draif, Hack, and Gravy got to the med bay, they could hear Leti.

"They're doing *what?* Are they insane? This is space! You don't just jump from ship to ship." Gravy turned tail and ran toward the commons.

Hack winced as he entered the room. He wished he could run. "It'll be fine, baby. You'll see."

"Don't you *baby* me," Leti said. He stood, Pepper strapped to his chest. His hands were on his hips and fire in his eyes. Damn, he looked good. "What about Beck and Selene? I know Draif and you are feeling guilty so you two will be idiots until Lucas is back, but what about the other two?"

Draif sent Hack a glare. "Hypocrite," he mumbled.

Hack smiled sweetly at the small man. So, yes, he did guilt-ridden, stupid shit all the time. That's why he could give a good pep talk about it.

"We want to go, Leti," Selene said. "Lucas is part of our crew." She paused and tilted her head in that weird, creepy doll way of hers. "If given the chance, would you go?"

"Well, of course I wouldn't… Damn it, fine. I would go in a heartbeat," Leti sputtered, then glared at Hack's smile. "Lucas is ours and those jerks deserve to be blown up."

Morrick smiled from his seat next to Alois's bed. "Here I thought you were a gentle and practical man."

Draif snorted and Hack laughed.

"Not when it comes to protecting others," Hack said. He walked to Cordelia's bedside and smoothed a hand over her blonde hair as she slept peacefully.

Morgan sat in the chair beside her bed, wounds bandaged and amusement twinkling in his eyes. Hack grabbed his head and kissed the top. "Eww, mama mode activated," Morgan groaned.

Leti tsked. "When you're injured, Morgan, you take the kisses." He walked over and kissed Morgan's head too. "Just take them."

Gods, Hack loved his mate.

Nettle laughed. "It's a proven fact that kisses solve all injuries." He handed a small bag to Draif. "You might need medical supplies for Lucas, and please, be careful.

Beck is great in a fight, but he isn't practical. I think it's all that creativity floating around in his big engineering brain."

Beck burst into the room.

"Come on, guys," he said enthusiastically, waving a mechanical flat disc. "I have this new gadget I want to try out."

"What's it do?" Selene asked.

"That looks kind of neat," Draif said.

"Idiots," Nettle mumbled. "You're all idiots."

The fourth and last clamp latched to the bottom of the Concord ship. Dannol flew the Blue Solace beneath the larger ship, perfectly and smoothly matching their speed. The Havenite had serious skills.

Dru's voice came through the comm. "You all are good to go. Make it quick. Draif and Beck up first."

Leti made sure Draif's helmet was secure and then checked Beck's. "You two be careful. We want Lucas back, but we don't want to lose you all too."

"Yes, sir," Beck said, grinning and saluting.

Finn laughed from beside him and Leti snorted. "Get going, doofus."

The two men entered the space lock, depressurized, then hooked up to the cable, climbing over to the other ship. They entered it without issue, disappearing from sight.

"You two are next," Dru said. "Wait one minute, then go."

Leti patted Selene on the shoulder and hugged Hack one last time. "Please be careful, you two. I know that this is technically a good idea, but it's also a really bad idea. A lot could go wrong, fast. You have your locators on, right? In case you disconnect from either ship?"

"Yes, baby. We're good. Don't worry," Hack said. He gave Leti one last kiss and put his helmet on. The bombs were strapped to Selene and Hack's fronts for easy access.

"I'll be here when you get back."

"Good to go, guys," Dru said.

The two quickly left the ship, each following a different hook. Leti watched out the window, stroking Pepper's head as she slept. The two both clamped onto the enemy ship, then began to move toward their target spots.

"So far, so good," Finn said. The two went surprisingly fast, considering they were hanging from a ship mid-flight.

"How can something that's happening so fast feel like it's happening in slow motion?" Leti unstrapped Pepper when she woke up, pulling her bottle out of her bag.

Finn shrugged. "Stress and tension. All our missions feel like this, even though they're not usually as action packed as you would think."

"What do you mean?"

"Most of the time we're doing security reviews, escorting Charybdis Station officials, or hauling goods around."

"Mercenaries do that?"

"We do. Honestly, we're not really mercenaries anymore. Charybdis Station started out as an independent mercenary group, but that was over six hundred years age. Now, it's like a planet. We have our political alliances, trade agreements, etc., etc." He shrugged. "Don't get me wrong, we also have the standard rescue mission, siege break, or bounty collection. That just happens less than you would think."

"I've been thinking about how to do this," Leti said, nodding to Pepper. "I want to be with Hack all the time, but what about Pepper and Mo?"

Finn looked thoughtful. "The captain will probably end up changing our routes to short trips that are closer to home. There's a lot of work in our system, but the captain's been weird the last year or so. He's gone for jobs far from home. Now that he has you and a couple of kids to think of, he'll change things up a bit." He smiled. "It will be a damn good thing too. Dru wants to be closer to her husband and most of the others miss home more and more."

"Damn right, I miss my man," Dru said from the comm on the wall, startling Finn and Leti. "Vid-screen sex can only last a girl so long."

Leti laughed while Finn groaned.

"I didn't need to know what you and Lerais get up to, damn it," Finn said.

"That man," Dru moaned. Finn gagged and covered his ears. "Uh oh, we've hit a snag, guys," Dru said, all seriousness.

"Draif is bringing Lucas over, but we need Medical waiting. I'll send Nettle." Silence for a moment. "He's on his way. Finn, go prepare a couple of cells. They are bringing some company with them and say they're not mercs, but the Concords can be tricky. We'll isolate them until we get the full story. Morgan and Ava will help with the new company."

"Got it," Finn said, racing off. "Be right back, Leti."

Leti watched as the docking entrance opened and Draif attached to the line. He pulled a limp body in a spacesuit behind him. The suit looked funny though. One leg wasn't filled out like the rest.

Nettle and Juniper came in with a gurney. The cook was Fallon and very similar in coloring to Ava. He seldom left the kitchen or commons, but Hack said he always helped when needed, never hesitating. Worry lined the golden man's face.

"They making it okay?" Nettle's voice shook. "Dru, did they say anything about what injuries he has?"

"Nothing yet, Nets," she answered. "Just said he needed Medical pronto."

"They're almost here," Leti said.

Juniper moved to the window. "What's wrong with the leg in that suit?" Finn, Ava, and Morgan came into the room, Morgan still limping, face pale.

Draif entered through the space lock. "He's missing a leg and has a shit-ton of injuries. We patched him up enough to travel, but I think moving hurt him even more," Draif said.

"Get the suit off and get him on the gurney," Nettle ordered. Everyone reacted immediately, helping to move Lucas and pulling at the suit. The more of Lucas that was revealed, the angrier Leti got. He was in enemy hands for a total of an hour and a half. They had done all of this in that short time?

Lucas's left leg was gone from mid-thigh down. A makeshift bandage covered the end. His right arm looked like ground meat, skin hanging off and bones peeking out. He had another bandage covering one eye, but blood continued to leak from beneath. Those were the worst injuries, but he was naked and covered in wounds and burns.

Nettle whimpered as they moved him to the gurney. "Our poor Lucas. Has he been sedated or is he just unconscious from pain?"

"Sedated," Draif answered. "A mild one, but it was all we could find." He removed his helmet, his misery plain on his face. "They only had him a little over an hour."

"The Concords are fucking monsters," Finn spat out.

"Let's move," Nettle said, once Lucas was strapped in. "Fast but gentle."

Nettle and Juniper carried Lucas out.

Draif took a deep breath and slowly let it out. "We have more of the Concords' prisoners coming. The guards were passed out drunk after having 'fun' with Lucas. The few that weren't, well, Beck's new toy really is awesome. Right now, we have all their prisoners in the hallway outside the room we came in. I need to get back over to help Beck before they're discovered. How many suits do we have? Can any of you help?"

"We have eleven suits here, counting Lucas's but it's bloody," Ava said.

"They won't care," Draif said.

Leti took a breath. Time to be a mercenary. "Ava, stay here to help pull them in and provide first aid. Morgan, you're still wounded from the earlier fight. Take Pepper and keep things organized. Finn, you and I will suit up and get moving. How many are left, Draif?"

"Damn it, Leti, I am not letting you go out the space lock. Hack will kill me," Dru said.

"Dru, there are injured people over there that need our help before we blow these fuckers up. I'm going," he said and handed Pepper and her bag to a shocked Morgan.

"Fuck, fuck, fuck," Dru said through the comm. "Morgan, you and Pepper come to the bridge and run things from here. Hack and Selene still have about half the bombs to place, but they're making good progress. Dannol's rocking it, but he knows to tell you if things get too hard." She walked into the room. "Let's move assholes." She tossed Leti a suit. "Make sure to grab a locator too, just in case."

Long before he was ready, Leti was slowly moving between the ships with a thin spacesuit between his skin and either an icy, painful death from exposure to space, or the hot, fiery one from the two ships' engines. Oh gods, what was he *thinking*? He squeezed his eyes shut for a moment and kept moving forward. At the door to the battleship, Draif hooked a second line to the ship.

Dru's voice came through his helmet. "Grab a prisoner, transfer to the second line and go. Some are good to pull themselves. Just get the ones who can't. One big circle, guys. Let's move."

Leti had an armful of half-filled spacesuit in a matter of seconds. A young blue face stared back at him, big grey eyes full of pain and fear, tears trickling down her cheeks. Leti gripped the child tighter and moved quickly back to the Blue Solace. He made the trip four times, two more children and an unconscious young woman. All had been non-human, leading him to wonder what the fuck the Concords were doing.

Ava pulled the woman from his arms. "One more trip, then Beck will bring the last over with him. Good work, sugarplum."

The last was another woman, but there was no fear in her eyes, just disdain on her very human face. He pulled her close and moved back to the ship. Hack waited for him there, eyes full of anger and worry, staring at him through the window. As soon as he was in the door, and the woman out of his arms, Hack pulled him out of the room.

"What the fuck were you thinking?"

Leti arched a brow, staring his angry mate down. "I was thinking that there were injured people who needed help. I was thinking that if they had done all that damage to Lucas in an hour and a half, imagine what they could have done to those others." He paused, standing on tiptoes to stare up at Hack. "I was thinking of what my mate would do in my place."

Hack's anger disappeared, and he buried his face in

Leti's neck, pulling him close. "Fuck, baby, you scared the shit out of me. You aren't a soldier. I didn't think you'd do something like that." He gave a weak laugh. "I should have known though. Only four days, but I *know* you."

"Pepper's with Morgan in the bridge," Leti said. "I made sure she was safe."

"Of course, you did." Hack smiled. "I'm not going to apologize for getting mad. My heart's still beating too fast."

Leti kissed his chin then stepped back. "I won't ask you to apologize for getting mad. It's going to happen often, I think." He grinned and turned to the chaos surrounding them. "I'll help get the wounded to the medical bay. No way are we putting them in the cells Dru had Finn get ready." He nodded to his mate. "Go blow the fuckers up."

"My pleasure," Hack said.

In all, they brought thirty-two additional people from the other ship. Most were children, but a few were young men and women. All but one were non-human and injured.

The human woman stood to the side and watched as the others were evaluated, patched up, and either sent to the med bay, or, if not too injured, somewhere to rest.

"Are you hurt?" Leti decided to give her the benefit of the doubt. She looked like a suspicious, bitchy person, but he could be wrong. She had been held prisoner on a mercenary ship after all. That had to be traumatic.

"Do I look injured, idiot?" The woman rolled her eyes and turned away from him.

Okay, so she *was* a suspicious, bitchy person.

Leti went over to the other prisoners, and the little blue girl he had carried over first limped to his side. She clung to Leti's leg, sucking her thumb. She looked to be about four years old. Her black hair was a mass of tangled and dirty curls, but he saw the hint of small, curved horns poking through. She was from Siren's Lament, like Selene.

He bent down and pulled her up and into his arms. She wrapped her arms around his neck and her legs around his waist. She whimpered and laid her head on his shoulder.

"Hey, sweetie," Leti said. "Do you hurt somewhere? What's your name?"

The little girl pulled her thumb from her mouth. "Rizzie," she whispered. "Leg hurts."

"Well, Miss Rizzie, let's get someone to check out your leg, okay?" Leti said. He carried her to the med bay and over to Morrick who had just finished applying antibacterial healer to a young Dedril woman.

"This is Dr. Morrick. He's helping out in the med bay today. Let's get him to look at your leg, sweetie." Leti tried to set her on a chair, but she started crying.

"Want to stay with you," she whimpered, and Leti's heart melted.

"Oh, baby girl, I'll stay right here with you." Leti sat in the chair and perched her on his lap.

Morrick smiled gently. "Which leg is hurting, little miss?" Rizzie pointed to the right one, thumb back in

her mouth. "Okay, let's see what the scanner says." He ran it over her leg and looked at the readout for a few moments. "It was broken, but not set. It healed back wrong, and now the bones are grinding together. I imagine it hurts quite a bit. She'll need a small surgery to fix it."

Leti kissed her head. "Can we do that now or is it too busy?"

Morrick thought for a moment. "When you're done helping, why don't you take her to your room, give her a bath and a hot meal. Once she's gotten a good night's sleep, we'll get the leg fixed. That will give us time to tend to the more urgent injuries and her time to adjust."

"Good plan," Leti said. "How's Lucas?"

"Nettle has been working on him since bringing him in. It's touch and go. I don't know if he's going to make it, Leti," Morrick said, eyes sympathetic.

Leti hugged Rizzie close and shut his eyes. He could still see the man working with Draif in the training room, his face focused and grave. Lucas was a Betonize-Cardinal hybrid. He had a pair of silky brown ears and a matching tail, like a Cardinal, but the fangs, black eyes, and large size of a Betonize. He looked scary as hell, but he had been gentle and kind to Draif.

"What about Alois? How is he doing?"

"There is some good news there," Morrick said. "His vitals have picked up. He's still unconscious and apt to stay that way for a while, but it's a healthy unconscious, as strange as that sounds."

A few tears trickled down Leti's cheek. "Thank the

gods. That's something at least." He picked Rizzie up in his arms. "I see Cordelia is awake. I have someone I want you to meet, sweetie."

Cordelia looked very groggy, but conscious. Biscuit curled against her side, adoring eyes locked on her face. "Leti, I just woke up. What's happening?"

Leti set Rizzie on the side of her bed and gave the quick version of events. "Do you feel up to watching my new friend for me? You don't need to be up and about quite yet, and Rizzie needs to rest too."

Cordelia smiled at the little girl. "Will you be my resting buddy? I'll tell you about our friend Selene. She's a Siren, like you." Rizzie looked uncertain, so Cordelia said, "I might need some help petting Biscuit too. I don't know if I can do it on my own."

"Okay," Rizzie said, then looked back at Leti. "Daddy Leti, you'll come back, right?"

Cordelia's wide eyes met his, and she mouthed *Daddy Leti?*

Leti shrugged, heart beating fast. "I will definitely be back, Rizzie girl," he said. He leaned down and whispered to Cordelia. "Ask her about her parents."

He helped Rizzie lean back in Cordelia's arms, kissed her forehead, then grinned and kissed Cordelia's too. "Be good, girls."

Cordelia rolled her eyes and waved him off, attention turning to the little girl. Leti hurried back to the space lock and the other former prisoners.

HACK AND SELENE watched the bombs charge. Two more minutes and they were good to go. Hack held Pepper in his arms, rocking her softly. Morgan sat in the co-pilot chair, still pale and weak, with a little bit of baby puke on him.

Dannol had already detached from the ship and was flying at a safe distance behind it. Hector perched on the back of his chair, watching the ship in front of them. Gravy sat at Hack's feet and Fluffle draped along Selene's shoulders.

Hack suddenly started laughing.

Selene looked at him, eyes flat. "Why are you laughing?"

"Yeah, Captain," Dannol said with a giggle. The man couldn't help but laugh when someone else did. "This is an important moment."

"You have a rooster on the back of your chair. I have a dog at my feet, and Selene has a cat on her shoulders. I know somewhere on this ship, Dru is wearing a newt. Fuck, the thing rode in her spacesuit when they were rescuing people. Biscuit's probably still with Cordy. We are covered in pets. The big bad mercenaries all have cute and cuddly pets."

"Speak for yourself, Captain," Morgan grumbled. "I didn't get one. The llama's cute and all, but it's not a cat or dog, and I'm not going near Leti's fucking dragon. Damn thing hisses at me every time I pass it in the hall."

Dannol laughed at him. "Your reputation can take it, sir. We're still fierce, I promise."

"Yeah, well, the galaxy's going to have to get used to

it. I won't give any of it up." He looked at the timer. "Almost time."

The doors opened, and Leti helped a young Wello woman into the bridge. "Will, can Lilah watch the ship blow up?"

The woman was covered in scars, wounds, and burns from her face to her bare feet. She was also pregnant, close to birth if Hack was correct. Leti's eyes were green steel when they met his.

"She's wants her baby to know for sure that its sperm donor is gone. That he can't hurt them."

Hack helped her to the captain's chair. "Here's a front row seat, ma'am. Dannol's seen no pods leave."

"Thank you," she said. Her voice was raspy, barely above a whisper.

"It's time," Selene said.

When the timer hit zero, the explosions began. The back of the ship went first, bursting into pieces, and then the explosion spread through the rest. The Concords' battleship painted a beautiful picture across the black void of space, a lovely burst of metal and bolts.

Hack finished updating the admiral. "We scavenged the remains, but not much was left." He rocked Pepper's carrier on the desk.

"Gods, a simple mission turned complicated quick."

"Yeah," Hack said. "I haven't made it to my room yet tonight. The fucking water has gotten very muddy. The crew is still tending to the survivors. I'll check in once things are taken care of."

"Coming home now?"

"We're going to stop at Union Station to pick up the element. Morrick said the young man that has it will only give it to him. Then we'll head home with our refugees." Gravy rested his head on Hack's knee, and he ran his fingers over the dog's silky ears.

"Have you spoken with them? Do they have families to contact? We can start the process here."

"I just sent you a list of the names, species, and last known locations that we have so far. We're still compiling it though. Many of them are children who were either captured with their parents who were tortured and killed first, or they were sold by their parents. I worry that there won't be a place for most of them to go."

"You know we'll take care of them." Charybdis Station always did. They took in anyone who agreed to follow the rules, tolerate others, and keep the peace.

"Can you get the Yellow Solace to do the security review job? I have a feeling we need to get this element and get the fuck out of Dodge."

"It's done. I already reassigned it."

Hack grinned. "You want to meet Leti, don't you?"

The admiral looked sheepish. "Is that so wrong? He sounds wonderful."

"He floated between two ships moving at high speeds in space to help injured people. He's going to drive me crazy."

"Crazy?" Leti's voice came from behind him. "I'm going to drive you crazy, am I?"

"Uh oh," the admiral said, grinning. "Someone's in trouble."

Hack turned his chair and there was his mate, expression fierce and eyes dancing with mischief. A little blue Siren was perched on his hip. She looked freshly bathed and was wearing one of his black t-shirts. She had oversized, fuzzy penguin socks on her feet. Hack reached out and pulled his mate and Leti's little friend into his lap.

"Baby, you drive me the best kind of crazy," he said and kissed his neck. The little girl giggled, thumb stuffed in her mouth.

"Smooth, Will." His dad laughed. "So, this is Leti, my new son?"

Leti blushed and grew shy right before Hack's eyes. "Hi, sir. It's nice to meet you."

"Gah, sir!" Fasi laughed again. "No need for that. You can either call me Dad or Fasi, whatever makes you comfortable. Renee and I are looking forward to meeting you. Mo's still a bit of a mystery, but when I started telling him about all your pets, he came out of his shell. Couldn't get him to stop asking questions."

Leti grinned. "Good. I can't wait to meet him and his rabbit. When you speak to him next, make sure you tell him he has two little sisters now too."

"Two?" Fasi and Hack asked at once.

"Yes, this here is Rizzie. She's our daughter. Her bio-bastards sold her to the Concords because she can't sing. I'm not sure of the significance of that, but we don't want to talk about them, do we sweetie?" Leti whispered something in the girl's ear and she laughed loudly.

"Daddy Will, you gonna read my bedtime story?"

His dad's eyes grew wet. "Daddy Will? I need to move your shi… stuff to a four bedroom."

Hack slowly closed his mouth and stood, setting Leti and Rizzie down. He went to the closet of his office and pulled out a large, fluffy purple object. He crouched in front of Rizzie.

"When I was about your age, my dad found me just like Daddy Leti and I have found you." He pointed to the screen and Rizzie waved at the admiral. "My new mom, your new grandma, gave me this and told me that it would comfort and protect me as long as I had it, just like she would. See, it's purple, just like your grandpa. He can change into a wolf too."

Rizzie's eyes grew big. "Really?"

"Yep. It's stayed with me for a long time. Sometimes, when I'm sad or scared, it still makes me feel better."

He handed her his purple wolf. "I want you to have it now, since you're my daughter. It'll protect and comfort you, just like it did me." Rizzie took it and hugged it tightly, smiling at Hack, big gray eyes full of adoration. "Of course, Daddy Leti and I will also protect and comfort you."

"What's his name, Daddy Will?"

"Milo, after my bio papa," he said. "I never told my new dad, but I knew my first papa would have been so happy that he found me, that my dad could take care of me when my papa couldn't anymore."

"Oh, Will," his dad said, voice cracking. "You're making me fuc… freaking cry, you jerk."

"Thank you, Daddy Will," Rizzie said. "I'll take good care of him and love him and snuggle with him and make sure Princess Buttercup doesn't eat him."

"Good, so you've met Princess too, huh?" Hack gently picked her up.

"Owie," she cried.

Hack froze. "What's wrong, ladybug?"

"My leg hurts. Netsie and Morry's gonna fix it tomorrow though."

"Oh, good. Let's get you to bed so you get plenty of sleep for tomorrow, huh?"

"Okay. My bed's by Pepper's, so I can watch my little sister."

Hack carried Rizzie out of the room, followed by Gravy, as the little girl rambled away and hugged her wolf.

THE ADMIRAL TURNED his wet eyes to Leti. "You are a wonder, my boy, an absolute wonder."

Leti blushed. "I'm nothing special, si… um, *Fasi*, trust me." He shrugged and sat at Hack's desk. "So, my new friend Lilah told me that she heard a lot of the Concords' ships captured or bought non-humans to 'play' with. She says that she heard they kept some onboard at all times to entertain their men and women." Fasi's face looked horrified. "Do you think that you can talk to the Charybdis admiral? Maybe let him know what's going on?"

Fasi grinned. "I can definitely let him know. We'll be arranging for the survivors on your ship to either reunite with family or be settled into new homes." His purple eyes grew wicked, reminding Leti of Hack's as he watched the Concords' ship blow up. "I'm thinking it's time to declare war on the Concords."

Leti frowned. "Are you sure the admiral will go for that? I mean, he's the leader of a whole station. It's like its own planet the way Hack describes it. Will he want to deal with the political fallout?"

Fasi snorted. "Trust me, he'll feel as strongly about it as you do. Charybdis Station prides itself on helping those in need, no matter what species. We may be mercenaries, but that is a term solely used because we accept payment for work."

Leti breathed a sigh of relief. "Thank you so much. I know Hack would have brought it up when he learned more about the survivors we have, but I couldn't stand the thought of waiting." He gave Fasi a shy look. "Can I ask you something kind of private? Since you said I'm your new son and all? Two things, really."

"Absolutely!"

"First, can you arrange for a call with Mo? I know that Will is nervous about meeting his brother, but I thought that if we started getting Mo used to our faces, the first meeting will go better."

"I think he would love that. Just make sure your dragon is included in the call," Fasi said.

"Like Princess would let us leave him out," Leti scoffed. He grew quiet and shuffled the papers in front of him.

"What do you need, son? I will do anything in my power for you."

"Do you know a lot about Wello hybrids?"

"That is one species that is well-known by all." Fasi laughed. "I think they've intermixed with every known humanoid species. Why?"

"So, I'm a Wello hybrid," Leti said slowly and stood. "My father was very unhappy about it and did his best to ignore it. That means I don't know a lot about my own biology. I looked things up, of course, and tried to talk to my doctor, but my father forbade him to discuss it."

"*Fuckhead.*" Fasi growled, then looked sheepish. "Not you, your bio father, who shall remain unnamed."

Leti giggled. "Anyway, Will and I were, um, well… intimate."

Fasi laughed. "I would hope so."

"Shortly after, this line showed up on my abdomen." Leti nervously drew up his sweater and pulled his pants down a bit, baring the long, vertical red line. "Is that normal?"

The large Grell looked thoughtful, but his eyes twinkled with mirth. "First, let me say that your sweater is quite fashionable. Llamas are very 'in' or so I hear."

Leti nodded. He was well aware that his sweaters were amazing. Everyone except Ava said so. This particular one reminded him of Wobble, so he loved it.

"Second, I think that we will need to find the largest quarters available on the station. You may very well adopt more children or pets before you get home. I mean, you're still a couple of weeks away, so who knows what will happen. I'll try to find two of the largest sets of rooms next to each other in case you need to expand."

"What are you saying? Besides being a little critical of my habit of collecting people and animals, which I know you secretly love. I see you watching Pepper here like you want to grab her and never let her go. Oh, and please make sure there's room for Alois and Lucas. Will and I will need to take care of them. Neither of them has family, you know, and they *will* be okay. I just know it. I do have some money set aside. Draif is investing a lot of it, but I can help if it's too expensive. Oh, and of course, Draif will need to be near us too, and don't forget Wobble. I need a little space for my llama... and maybe a goat, we'll see."

Fasi's booming laughter echoed in the room. "Oh gods, I love you, dearest boy. I will find the space somehow. Oh, and son, what I'm trying to say is... you're pregnant."

Leti said goodbye to Fasi and left the office in a daze with Pepper's carrier rolling in front of him. *She sure sleeps a lot,* he thought. Beck told him that for a while, babies just slept, pooped, and ate. Oh gods, babies. Hack would be so mad. They only just adopted Rizzie that very day and Mo and Pepper were already part of their family. Leti decided he wouldn't say anything about a goat. That might push Hack too far.

He made his way to the med bay with the thought of seeing if he could be of any help. Morrick was sleeping in the chair next to Alois, completely exhausted. Cordelia and Biscuit had already made it back to their own room, allowing another survivor to have a bed, since every bed was full. Most of the survivors were recovering from severe injuries.

Nettle walked around, checking on each patient. His movements were slow with exhaustion. Morgan and Draif sat in chairs next to Lucas, heads together, whispering. A few little ones sat in other chairs, curled up with blankets.

Leti had been shocked at the sheer number of children without parents or family to return to. He wanted to take all the orphans and hug them close, making them all his own. Fasi ensured him that there were plenty of families that would be happy to take them in, but Leti wanted them all, the ones he'd talked to and the ones he hadn't met yet. He would have to let them go though. He was having a baby. Oh gods.

The human woman rescued from the Concords stood in one corner, staring at Morrick. She seriously creeped him out, but he knew that he wasn't the best judge of character. His social skills were almost nonexistent.

"Do you need a chair? Would you like to rest? We have beds ready for you all." Leti smiled and hoped she wouldn't be a jerk.

"That's Dr. Morrick, isn't it?" The woman ignored his questions, her gaze intent on the scientist. "He's a scientist, not a medical doctor. Why is he bothering to help these creatures? His mind is one of the greatest in all the galaxies."

Leti tried to contain his anger. "He happens to think these *creatures* are important and should be helped."

"That's unfortunate," she said and finally turned to look at him, unimpressed with what she saw. "I'm Dr. Olivia Franklin. I've never worked directly with Dr. Morrick, but we study in the same field."

"Why were you with the Concord? You're not like the other prisoners."

"I would certainly hope not," she said and sniffed, casting a look of contempt around the room. "They took me from my home this morning and told me there was a very important project I was needed for. I wasn't given the opportunity to say no, but I was allowed to pack a bag. Of course, it's gone now that you just *had* to blow up the ship."

"Okay, see you later, lady," Leti said and walked away, rolling Pepper with him. He plopped down in the seat next to Lucas. "How's he doing?"

Draif smiled and pulled Pepper out of her carrier, gently holding the baby to him. "He's still alive, which is good."

"It really is though," Morgan said. "After working on him for hours, Nettle said that he at least stands a chance at making it now."

"That's good news," Leti said. "He's a fighter, right? He'll do his best to come back from this."

"He's missing an eye and a leg, and Nettle had to amputate his damaged arm. Why would he want to fight to get better?" Draif asked, clearly upset. "He said he loved being a mercenary, perfecting his battle techniques. What will he do if he wakes up?"

"The station will set him up with a robotic arm and leg. They have the most advanced mechanical prostheses in the galaxy. The eye will be a little harder, but they've made a lot of advances there since I last checked," Morgan said. "He'll have to adjust to them, but I know plenty of guys with robotic body parts that fight just as good, or even better, than they did before."

"Really?" Draif asked, wet eyes hopeful.

"Yeah, man," Morgan said, giving him a one-arm hug. "This sucks, big time, but it's not the end of the world for him."

"There's no reason for you to feel guilty either,

Draif," Leti said softly. "This isn't your fault, and he'll tell you that too once he wakes up."

Morgan slapped the back of Draif's head. "You've been feeling guilty? Over this? Shit happens, Draif. You are not at all at fault here."

Draif frowned and rubbed his head. "Okay, okay, I hear you."

Leti chuckled and stood. "Give me my Pepper. I'm going to check in with Alois." Leti and Pepper went to the unconscious Dedril. Morrick was starting to wake up, still groggy.

"Leti, how are you?"

He smiled at the scientist and shrugged. "Better than most. How's Alois?"

"His vitals have improved, and his wound is starting to heal. Nettle was quite pleased when he checked on him earlier. I've been trying to stay with him so he's not alone."

"Verion, you have to be tired. Why don't you go get some sleep?"

"I might be needed here. Besides, I usually sleep at my desk, so this chair is actually a lot more comfortable than I'm used to." He raised his eyebrows and stared hard at Leti. "Now, you called me out on my nonsense this morning, so it's my turn. What's wrong?"

"Ugh, fine." Leti gave in easily. He was dying to talk to someone. "So, Will and I met like four days ago, right?"

"So I heard from Cordelia and Nettle."

"I have Pepper, my little sister, who I care for, so she's part of the family. Then, Will just found out, like, yesterday that he has a half-brother waiting on him back home. Of course, Mo is part of our family too, right?"

"I don't see the problem, Leti. You have a huge heart. I know there's room in there for everyone."

"Yes, there is. I have Wobble and Princess Buttercup too, and Will has Gravy."

"Okay, I still don't see the problem."

"This morning, we adopted Rizzie. She's a little Siren that came from the other ship. I carried her over."

"I remember her. She's a sweetheart and I know she was quite attached to you. Did the captain not want to adopt her? Did he give you trouble?"

"No, he was great. He is officially her favorite person now."

"Are you jealous?"

"No, I'm pregnant."

"What? Already?" Morrick started to laugh. "Oh, I see now. You have to tell your mate that you're going to have another baby after he's already been surprised with three."

"Yes. He's going to hate me, isn't he?" Leti groaned and plopped into a seat.

"I seriously doubt that. Your mate is crazy about you. He'd have to be to not run screaming when he saw your dragon. Gods, man, that thing is huge... and grumpy. It hissed at me earlier."

Leti laughed. "Okay, maybe you're right. I'll take it one day at a time." He smiled fondly at the scientist. "By the way, we appreciated having you today, Verion. All these people you helped… I think your son would have enjoyed seeing it."

Morrick smiled, eyes joyful. "Do you think so? He certainly would have been useful to have around today, right?" He paused a moment, deep in thought. "I think I will contact him, like you suggested, when all this mess with the element is over. Maybe he'd like to come visit Charybdis Station."

"I think that if he's half as smart as you say he is, then he will."

Nettle sat across from him, pulling Leti's leg up into his lap. "I've been meaning to remove your cast since yesterday. I swear when it rains, it pours."

Leti had almost completely forgotten his ankle. It hadn't bothered him for the past couple of days. Nettle made quick work of Leti's thin cast, then leaned back, eyes closed. He was snoring a second later, Leti's foot still propped in his lap.

"I really think you all could use Wyatt's help on the ship," Morrick said with a chuckle.

LETI PAUSED in the doorway of the commons and looked around. Crewmembers mixed with recovering survivors. Food covered almost every table and Porkchop ran around, begging food from each child he came across. The little ones just giggled and pinched off pieces for him.

Juniper walked from table to table, checking on everyone. The man's butterscotch skin flushed deeply with each compliment he received for his food. He smiled when he saw Leti and waved him to a table where Selene sat, alone, with Fluffle draped across her shoulders.

"Hey, Selene," Leti said, sitting down. "Everything looks in order with the survivors. How are you doing?"

"I'm fine," she said flatly, popping an olive in her mouth. "Remember, tomorrow we have another lesson scheduled."

"I'll be there," Leti replied.

Juniper stopped by and placed a plate of warm pot roast in front of him. "Here's dinner, Leti."

"This looks and smells so good, Juniper," Leti said, his face inches from the savory dish. "I think I love you."

Juniper laughed. "Are you talking to me or the pot roast?"

"The pot roast of course," Leti said, grinning. He dug in, moaning at the wonderful taste. "I might love you too though."

Juniper laughed again and moved to the next table, Miss Speckles following him. The chicken usually was in her nest or following Juniper. There was no doubt Leti had truly lost another pet.

After eating his dinner at an embarrassing speed, he turned back to Selene. "Can I ask you a question, Selene? About Siren's Lament?"

She stiffened but nodded.

"Rizzie says her parents sold her to the Concords because she couldn't sing. What the hell does that mean? I guess it's important since they went to such extremes, but I don't understand."

Selene was quiet for a moment, then spoke. "There is a faction of very old, very traditionalist Sirens on Siren's Lament. They believe that their people should follow the old ways." She picked up another olive, popping it in her mouth. "When humans first settled on Siren's Lament, they were entranced with the native Sirens. It eventually became the reasoning behind the human name for the planet."

"So singing is part of a Siren's life, like in the Old-Earth myths?"

"Yes and no. Those first interactions with humans were… deadly for the humans. A Siren's voice can manipulate a person, daze their mind and control them. Humans kept coming, though, and eventually intermixed with the natives. The traditionalists believe that Sirens should remain as pure of blood as possible and use their abilities to control the planet and perhaps, eventually, the system."

Leti couldn't hide his dismay. "That sounds a lot like the Concords."

"Yes. The difference is that the traditionalists are a very small faction. Most of the population of Siren's Lament are modern thinkers. Still, singing is seen as very special. If someone is born into a traditionalist family and can't sing…" She paused for a moment. "It's not at all uncommon for those children to disappear. Rizzie's family sold her because she was not 'Siren' enough for their beliefs."

"That's horrible," Leti said sadly. "You said it's not even uncommon?"

"No. That is how I ended up on Charybdis Station."

"You can't sing?"

"I can sing, but it never turns out correctly. They tried and tried to train me, but it proved impossible. Not that I would want to control a person's mind anyway."

"I'm sorry that they couldn't see your true worth, Selene. I'm not sorry you're here with us though."

"Thank you. I enjoy my life with the Blue Solace."

Leti smiled, and the two talked for hours before Leti remembered the scheduled call with Mo.

"I'll see you tomorrow, Selene," he said, leaving and rushing to his room. Hack was already there, putting a fresh diaper on Pepper, while Rizzie sat on her bed, chattering away.

They gathered at the end of the bed, across from the vid-screen, for their first call with Mo. The call had an awkward start. Both Hack and Mo were shy of one another. The long silences were starting to really bother Leti, but when Princess crawled into Leti's lap, Mo became a little chatterbox.

"This is Abbot," Mo told them, holding the fat, brown jack rabbit up so they could all see. He looked about ten pounds and was more than a handful.

The boy was tall and gangly, too skinny by far. His black hair, golden skin, and tattoos matched Hack's spot on. That mischievous glint in his black eyes also matched Leti's mate.

"He's a handsome fella, Mo," Leti said. "What does

he eat? I've always wanted a rabbit, but they are actually hard to come by on Vextonar."

"He eats anything plant-based. Back home, he ate cacti, brush, even sticks."

"How'd you get him," Rizzie asked, pulling her thumb from her mouth. She sat on Hack's lap, bundled up in one of Leti's favorite quilts.

"I was hunting one day with Grandpa Moses and I saw a hawk dive down and grab this adult rabbit. Abbot was her baby and was the only one left," Mo said. "Grandpa said that he was too small to skin, but I felt really bad for him. I snuck him in my shirt and took care of him in secret for a while. I'm basically his mama."

"You a good mama?" Rizzie giggled and hugged Hack tightly.

"The best mama," Mo said and grinned. "Do you have a pet, Rizzie? Who is that big, furry monster sitting next to you?"

"That's Daddy Leti. He not that furry," she said and laughed loudly. Mo joined in, face lighting up.

"Ha, ha, little lady," Leti said, trying to keep a straight face. Hack didn't even try, booming with laughter. "That big, furry monster would be Gravy. He's been guarding the girls, but he worships your brother." He sighed. "There was a time when I had ten pets, plus my Druffle. Now, I'm down to two pets and half my Druffle."

"I'll share Abbot with you, Uncle Leti," Mo said, smiling shyly. "I can help you take care of Princess Buttercup too. He looks awesome."

"Finally! Someone appreciates my sweet, baby boy," Leti said, hugging Princess and kissing his scaly head.

LETI BREATHED HARD, groaning, as Hack pounded deep into him from behind. The shower poured down on the two of them and masked the sounds they made. His mate held him from behind, face burrowed into his neck.

"Leti," Hack moaned, coming hard.

Leti's cum painted the side of the shower. Gods, the things his mate did to him. Hack gently pulled out of him and cleaned them both up. He turned Leti around and kissed him deeply.

"I love you, baby," Hack whispered.

"I love you too, Will," Leti said sadly. "There's something I need to tell you, though, and I really hope you don't get mad."

"What's wrong? Did you go outside the ship again? Damn it, Leti!"

"No," Leti said, rolling his eyes. "Why would I just randomly go floating around outside the ship?"

"Maybe you saw a space otter," Hack said.

Leti's eyes widened and he gasped. "There are space otters?" He wanted one and he wanted it right now.

"No," Hack said, laughing. "But if there were, you would go outside the ship to get it."

"You suck." Leti pouted. Hack wrapped him in his arms and kissed the top of his head as Leti stewed in his anger. A space otter sounded awesome.

"You are so adorable," Hack said, smiling. "So, what's wrong then? You'd have to… I don't know… kill someone for me to be mad at you, then I *still* probably wouldn't get mad since they'd likely deserve it."

"I'm pregnant," Leti said and held his breath, waiting for Hack's reaction.

Hack stared at him in shock. Slowly, a grin appeared. "Are you serious? For real?"

"Yes, Will, I'm serious," Leti said, hope filling him. "I take it by that smile, you're okay with the idea? Even though we only just adopted Rizzie?"

"Of *course*, I'm okay with it," Hack said. He grabbed Leti up and spun him around the shower. "We're having a baby!"

"We *have* a baby, Will, and we have a four-year-old, and a teenager. Oh gods, we have a teenager."

"We'll be fine, baby," Hack said, setting him back down. "We got this."

The two dried each other off, laughing, petting, and kissing in the process. Leti peeked in on the girls. Pepper slept like a… well, like a baby. Leti leaned over and kissed her head.

Rizzie was asleep on her makeshift cot. Her little leg was propped up on a pillow and she snuggled Milo close, breathing softly. Leti pulled the blanket up a little more, tucking it around her.

Gravy slept between the two girls, so Leti stepped over him and went to bed. Princess lounged on one side of the bed, already snoring little puffs of smoke, and Hack lay on the other. He looked half asleep. He held out his arm and Leti climbed between them and curled up beside his mate.

Hack held him close, front pressed to his back, and smoothed a hand over Leti's belly. "I love you, baby. Oh, and you too, mate."

"Love you too, goofball," Leti said, full of peace and happiness. They'd make their family work. Just like that.

13

*A*fter three days of bliss spent with his mate and children, Hack and most of his crew were finally well-rested and recuperated from the battle on Frost Veil and the chaotic rescue of the Concord ship's prisoners. They docked at Union Station that morning, and he hoped to leave that afternoon so they could get Morrick and the element to the safety of Charybdis Station.

Alois was still unconscious, but Nettle thought he could wake at any time. Unfortunately, Lucas was awake and in a lot of pain. The med bay was out of pain medication and Nettle was afraid to keep him sedated. One of the crew sat with him at all times, but it was hard seeing their friend hurt so much. The pets had even started taking turns sitting with him, as if they understood what was happening. Fluffle did growl at him, but she still sat next to him, offering her warmth.

Now, Hack gathered in the conference room with

most of his crew, planning their outings. "We need medical supplies desperately," Nettle said. "We need to keep Lucas and Alois stable and most of the survivors need more help. Put simply, either we get more supplies, or we leave them here so they can get the care they need."

"With the Concords out for revenge, that's probably not a good idea," Dru said.

"Agreed," Nettle said. "I have a contact that can fill an order within a couple of hours."

"Alright," Hack said. "Nettle, you and Beck can take care of the supplies. I know you needed some things too, right Beck?"

"Yeah, we were already low on maintenance material, and with more people on board, we are running through what we have faster. Juniper could use more food too."

"Place the orders, have them delivered to the spaceport, and go get them. Then, get back here fast," Hack ordered. "The spaceport is well-guarded, anything outside of it isn't. You don't go down into the city, and you stay in crowded areas here." He thought for a moment. "Take Juniper with you. One more man can't hurt."

"We'll place the orders now," Nettle said, pulling out his tablet. Beck followed suit and began ordering what he needed.

"Morrick, where's this man we need to meet?" Dru pulled up a rough map of the city they were docked in. Union Station was a strange planet. Law and order weren't well kept outside the spaceports and there were quite a few seedy individuals running the larger cities.

"Sebastian's an indentured servant at a bar in the lower city. He can't come to us, but we can easily go to him."

"We need to plan for an ambush this time," Hack said. "I don't want to be caught unaware again. As soon as we docked, our ship's presence was registered, so it's just a matter of time before they come for us. Morrick, can you contact Sebastian, see if anything suspicious is going on at his end?"

"Of course, Captain," he said. "I'll step out now and check."

"Dru, I need you and Dannol to remain on board. Everyone else will be needed, but we have to protect the people on board too."

"I understand," Dru said. She wasn't pleased to be left behind again, but Hack knew she really did understand.

Morrick stepped back into the room. "Sebastian said that everything seemed calm on his end. He hasn't been followed and hasn't noticed any unusual people. No one has been by to ask about anything related to the element or Nina. He will only give it to me though. He said Nina was adamant about that." The scientist sank into his chair. "He heard that Nina died but was told that it was in a lab accident. He didn't take the truth that well. I think we may be smuggling out an indentured servant."

"Okay, we'll deal with that. He wants to fight, we'll let him fight. Let's hope that end of things will be easy." The Concords were more active right now and there were some openly-docked in the spaceport. His contact on the planet had given him the docking IDs and the number of mercs on each ship. What the Concords lacked in skill, they made up for in numbers.

"They'll come once we expose ourselves," Selene said. "They think we already have the element. That's what they want. It seems like Morrick is secondary. They'd like to have him, but will settle for the likes of that second-rate scientist we picked off their ship."

"Dr. Franklin?" Ava asked. "She is rather unpleasant, but I imagine she'd be an easier partner for them then our own Dr. Morrick. She hates non-human species."

"I've always heard great things about her brain, but nothing good about her personality," Morrick said.

"Alright. Ava and Morgan will go out first, scout around the city. We stay in contact at all times," Hack instructed. "Morrick, Finn, and I will take a speeder straight to Sebastian and get the element. No sense in fucking around. Selene, Cordelia, and Draif will follow at a distance and wait here, at this brothel." He pointed to the location on the map.

"Classy," Selene said, voice flat.

"Once the element is in our hands, my group will book it to the brothel. Then we all fall back to the ship." He looked around the room. "Any suggestions?"

LETI FINISHED CHANGING Pepper's diaper. He smoothed a hand over her soft tuft of hair and placed her back in the bassinet. He looked down at his little Siren, passed out in her bed. Her surgery earlier had gone well, but Nettle had decided to keep her sedated for a few hours while the cast seal settled in. Cordelia had brought Biscuit by, and the little dog curled up next to Rizzie, offering his comfort. Gravy sat on his haunches between the girls, guarding them while Hack was away.

"Lilah," Leti said, moving around the screen. The Wello woman sat at the table, eating a late breakfast. She was much improved from when she'd arrived, taking walks around the ship and helping Nettle in the med bay. She was really good with all the basic, necessary things that bogged Nettle down. He was talking about having her train as a nurse once her baby was born.

Today, she looked happy and at ease in new clothes gifted to her by Ava. She kept eyeing Princess, though, like he would attack at any moment.

"Would you mind staying here and watching the kids? I'd like to stay on the bridge while Will's gone. I want to know what's going on, and Dru's still mad at me, so I need to irritate her in person," Leti said.

"I would be happy to, but only if you take your dragon with you."

"Princess Buttercup is harmless, I promise."

"He keeps getting bigger and bigger," she said.

"He does seem to be like ten feet now. I've never seen him bigger, though, so you shouldn't worry too much." Leti leaned down and rubbed the dragon's belly. "He's my big baby boy. Aren't you? Aren't you a pretty boy?"

Lilah watched, disgusted. "The llama is quite nice, but this is just... no, I can't."

"Fine, I'll take him with me, even though this is his favorite naptime," Leti said, watching her for signs of sympathy or guilt.

"He can nap on the bridge." No guilt or sympathy at all.

Leti laughed and dug his phaser out of the table drawer next to the bed. "Come on, Princess. Lilah doesn't love you like I do."

"THERE ARE a few Concord mercs milling around the entrance to the spaceport, Captain," Ava said. "They know we're here, or they'd all be at the brothels, casinos, or bars."

"Well, there's a group here at the brothel," Morgan said. "Sebastian said there were a few at the bar too, right?"

"Yes," Hack replied, frustrated. "He said he noticed them at every bar he could check in the lower city."

"They're spread out everywhere, aren't they?" Ava's voice was strained. "How are we going to do this?"

"Fast is our only hope," Hack said. "Nettle, Beck, and Juniper are going to be as obvious as they can. While they're in the spaceport, they're safe. We'll sneak out around them, try to stay concealed, but we focus on fast."

"We're heading to the entrance now, Captain," Beck said through the comm. "We'll make a big deal of loading shit up. Give us twenty minutes."

The spaceport was huge, miles and miles long. Hack, Morrick, and Finn sat low in the speeder, idling a few docks down from their own. Twenty minutes later, they started toward the entrance.

Hack couldn't help but chuckle as he passed Beck, who was yelling at the man delivering his supplies. The little man yelled right back, not at all afraid of the huge Grell. Nettle tossed supplies, in apparent disgust, joining in the spectacle, while Juniper steadily loaded everything. They were definitely drawing the attention of the mercs at the entrance, though the spaceport guards kept them from coming too close.

Hack drove by, hidden behind a large crate carrier. Once they hit the streets, he sped up, moving as fast as possible in the crowded city. Selene's vehicle followed at a distance, pulling over at the brothel.

"Streets are clear to the bar, Captain," Morgan said.

"Sebastian is waiting for you at the corner of his street," Ava said. "It's as far as he's legally allowed to go."

"You up for smoothing over the ruffled feathers when we take him with us," Hack asked.

"It may cost us some credits, but I'll take care of it, Captain," Ava replied.

Hack stopped at a corner, and Morrick opened his

door. "Come on, Sebastian." A young human hybrid jumped into the back next to the scientist.

"You're sure it's okay to come with you?" Sebastian quickly handed over a bag, eager to be rid of the responsibility of carrying the element.

"We'll take care of it," Hack said, turning around and racing back toward the brothel.

"Captain, we have a problem," Ava said. "Over a hundred Concord mercenaries are gathered right outside the entrance to the spaceport. Guards don't look happy, but as long as they aren't inside the entrance, they won't touch them."

"Alternate entrances?"

"No, sir," she said.

"We also have about thirty coming out of the brothel," Morgan said. "Fuck, they've seen us, Captain."

"We're almost there, Morgan. Load up and start back to the spaceport. We'll drive through them. Beck, status?"

"Loaded up, sir. Nettle is headed back to the ship with the supplies. Juniper and I are at the entrance. It's not going to be easy, Captain. They have a couple of pulse cannons."

"My goodness, they're not even attempting to hide their intentions," Ava said. "I'm just inside the spaceport now, Captain. I have my rifle and a good perch."

"How'd you get through?" Beck sounded baffled.

"No one ever looks up," she said.

"Oh captain, my captain," Beck said, voice strangely happy. "We have some friends that want to play too."

"Hey there, Will," a familiar voice came through the comm. "Dad told me you might need some help. Green Solace and Yellow Solace are here. Crews are gathering up front. Get your ass here so I can meet my big brother's mate. Man's got to be insane."

"Cas?" Hack said, laughing. "Great timing, little brother."

"We're almost there," Morgan said. "Oh fuck, the pulse cannon. Abandon fucking ship!"

Hack could see the explosion from a block away. "Morgan, status? Morgan?"

"They jumped out of the speeder in time, Captain," Ava said. Hack could hear weapons firing through her comm. "This fight isn't going to be pleasant."

"Two minutes out."

"You'll have to jump too," she said. "They're out for blood. I think they'll just try to pick the element out of the rubble."

"On it. Everyone, activate your shields. Finn, you need to get Morrick and Sebastian to the spaceport. Be prepared to jump in one minute."

"Captain," Morrick said, handing a bag over the seat. "Take the element, just in case. It's better that they don't get me *and* the artifact."

"They won't get either," Sebastian said, pulling out a phaser. "I'm not the best shot, but I'll do my best, Dr. Morrick. Nina would expect it."

As soon as the speeder reached the spaceport, a large pulse was fired toward them. They opened the doors, jumping right before the speeder exploded in a fiery blast. Hack landed hard, shrapnel sinking into his face and arms. He got to his feet, firing his phaser and calling his fire to him. Mercenary after mercenary fell before him, but there were too many.

Finn and Sebastian had Morrick between them, pushing toward the ship. Hack felt despair overtaking him. There was a barrier of well over two hundred Concord mercenaries between them and the entrance. Selene's group was huddled together at the half-way point, locked in with their backs to a building to the right.

Hack could see his brother and his crew at the entrance, firing from behind a makeshift barricade. The large blue Grell hybrid was easy to spot. Beck, Juniper, and the spaceport guards were at the other side of the entrance, firing from behind their own barricade. The captain of the Yellow Solace and her crew struggled to push out from the middle of the entrance.

Ava sat atop the spaceport wall, attempting to clear a path for Finn and the other two men, but it wasn't working. Even with the guards' help at the entrance, there were too many of them.

Hack called his fire, burning brightly from within and lighting up his eyes. At least Leti and the kids were safe.

"What's happening, Dru?" Leti asked, heart in his throat as he listened to the noise of the battle through the comm.

"Fuck, this isn't good, Leti. There are a shit ton of Concords at the entrance. The spaceport guards, The Yellow Solace, and The Green Solace have thrown in with us, but that's still over two hundred to fifty, with more Concords still arriving."

The doors to the bridge opened and Lilah and five of the adult survivors ran in, two men and three women.

"Lilah said you might need help," one of the men said. "We don't know what's going on, but we know those are the fuckers that had us. Let us help."

"Dru? We have to go." Leti was already headed for the door, Princess on his heels.

"Fuck, fuck, fuck." Dru opened a cabinet and started tossing weapons to the five survivors. "You two, you're too injured to go into battle, so you stay here at the ship and guard it. It will be locked up, but if it opens and it's not us, it's up to you to stop them, got it?" The two women both nodded, determined and fearless.

"Lilah, who's with the kids?" Leti handed her two phasers. He looked to the side, movement grabbing his attention. Princess was getting bigger. He looked to be twelve feet now.

"We put all the children who can move in your quarters. Two of the older children are watching them. Two more of the older ones are in the med bay, doing what they can."

"You need to go there too. Keep an eye on the injured," Dru said. "Plus, you're pregnant, lady. The battlefield is no place to birth a baby."

Lilah snorted and nodded in agreement. "You're

probably right. Plus, that nasty dragon's fifteen feet now. You said he never went over ten." She split to go to the med bay, glaring accusingly at Leti as he and the others went to the cargo bay.

"I didn't lie, I promise," he said, following Dru around the corner. Leti knelt next to Princess. He was getting bigger and bigger. "What's wrong, baby boy? I have to go save Will and the others. Do you need a nap?" Princess turned his head, looking him in the eyes, a deep, rough rumbling coming from his chest. "Oh, you want to help rescue Will, huh? I knew you liked him."

"You two, position yourselves here." Dru pointed. "Dannol, someone needs to stay to fly the ship. Pilots don't leave the ship. Golden rule."

"No, damn it," Dannol said. "They need us, and I won't let them down."

The little Havenite looked fierce, his laid-back demeanor gone.

"Umm, I can actually fly," one of the survivors said. "I'm a beginner, but I could do it in a pinch."

Dru pointed to the door. "Get going. Be ready to lift off as soon as we get back. *If* we fucking get back."

The man left, running out the door.

"Gods, let's do this, I guess. Leti, if you die, I will fucking kill you," Dru said and passed shield buttons, bags of grenades, and pulse cannons to everyone. Monty perched on her head, ready to join the battle.

"I have my lucky baby bunny sweater on, and Selene gave me two lessons in shooting. I'll be just fine."

"If I thought you'd stay…" Dru sighed.

"I'm not leaving Will, not ever."

"Yeah, yeah. True love and all that shit. Let's go."

Leti paused, looking at his twenty-five-foot dragon. "Oh, my beautiful baby boy, are those wings?"

14

Hack panted, pain spreading from the shot in his arm. He set another mercenary on fire. Hack's group had managed to get to Selene's, but that was it. More Concord mercs had shown up. All that could be said of the battle was that no one from his crew was dead. Yet. Morgan was unconscious and every last one of them had some kind of injury.

"Hack," Cas said through the comm. "What are we going to do?"

Hack moved to position himself in front of a wounded Finn, firing at the incoming mercs. "You have to leave. Get the Blue Solace and get out of here. There's more coming from up the street. Make sure Leti gets to the station, alright? Make sure he gets to Mo. Take care of them, Cas."

"Enough of that shit, Will," Cas said, despair spilling into his words. "I'm not leaving you."

"Neither are we." The voice of the captain of the

Yellow Solace was tired but pissed off. Audre Shepard wasn't one to leave a person behind, Hack knew that.

"Morrick!" Sebastian yelled.

Hack pushed the mercenary he was fighting back, Selene immediately taking his place in holding the line. He ran to the scientist's side, sadness filling him at the sight. Morrick had been shot multiple times, and the light slowly drained from his eyes.

"Wyatt," he whispered, then his empty eyes stared up at the sky.

"Oh gods, why did he do that?" Sebastian knelt beside his body, cradling his head. "He saved me. I should've taken those shots. Gods, why?"

"Come on, Sebastian," Hack said, pulling the young man up. "We need you in the here and now. Grieve later."

"What the fuck?" Cas's voice came through the comm. "Uh, Will, you have incoming from above. It's… I don't know what the fuck it is."

"It's Princess Buttercup," Draif said. "Don't fire on him. He's a good guy… I think."

Hack looked up, jaw dropping at the twenty-five-foot-long, eight-foot-wide dragon flying over the Concords. His red scales gleamed, hard as metal as he flew low, blowing a wide wave of fire over the terrified enemy mercenaries, burning them alive. Their screams echoed against the walls of the city street.

The Charybdis mercenaries and spaceport guards whooped and cheered as they pressed the advantage, trying to keep the Concord mercenaries grouped together. Princess made two trips across the expanse of the Concords before Hack noticed the five figures on his back. They tossed grenades and fired pulse cannons into the enemies below.

"*Damn it*, Leti." Hack howled and a burst of his fire ignited two Concord men running around in the chaos.

"It's okay, Captain," Draif said. "He's wearing his lucky baby bunny sweater."

"It's Yusef the Terrible," Selene said. "I did give him a few lessons in shooting, Captain."

"I'm locking him in our room!" Hack roared.

"Your mate is kinda badass, big brother," Cas said, laughing. "He rode into battle on a dragon for you."

"My *pregnant* mate." Hack growled.

"Leti's pregnant? Gods, how many kids will you all end up with?" Draif couldn't keep the joy from his voice.

"Oh, pregnant mate flying on a dragon," Audre said. "Now I see why the stick's up your ass."

The Concord mercenaries ran in chaotic circles. Hack and Audre's crews cut them off from escaping into the city, while Cas's crew, Beck, and the guards held the line at the spaceport entrance. Within minutes, all the Concords were either dead or dying.

Princess landed in the middle of the battlefield and began to chew on a dead Concord merc.

Leti and the others slid off his back. He ran around Princess and yelled at the dragon, hitting his large snout with the end of his pulse cannon. "No, Princess, no! Spit that out. We do not eat people, baby boy. Spit it out right now!"

Princess looked at Leti, mouth full, then opened his jaws, body parts spilling onto the ground. The dragon whined and butted his head against Leti.

"Of course, you aren't in trouble, my sweet baby boy. You just can't eat people." Leti rubbed his head and cooed softly.

The Charybdis mercenaries and the spaceport guards stared at Leti and Princess in disbelief and a little fear. Dru, Dannol, and the two survivors remained at Leti's side, keeping an eye on the fallen mercenaries.

Draif and Hack reached Leti at the same time. Hack opened his mouth to start yelling, but he suddenly had an armful of mate.

"Is everyone alright? We passed Nettle on the way out. He's bringing the gurneys for the wounded. Where are you hurt, Will? Do you need immediate attention? Draif, what about you?"

Hack sighed and pressed his forehead to his mate's. "Leti, everyone is wounded. This... this could've been our deaths. Why, gods, why didn't you stay on the ship?"

Draif snorted. "Lucky baby bunny sweater seriously rocks, Leti." He started scratching Princess's head and muttering compliments. "Who's the best dragon in all the galaxies?"

"I made you a promise, Will. Do you remember? When you told me about your bio mother," Leti said.

"Leti..."

"I will *never* leave you behind. Not as long as there is a breath left in me. There is no life without you in it."

He kissed Hack, lips soft and sweet. "Now, is everyone alright?"

Draif hugged Leti from behind, standing on tiptoes to put his head on Leti's shoulder. "Leti, Morgan got bashed on the head and everyone's injured, but... Dr. Morrick didn't make it."

"What? Verion? What do you mean?"

Leti shoved out of their arms and began looking for the scientist. When he spotted him, he ran. Sebastian knelt next to Morrick, crying. Leti fell to his side.

"What happened?"

"My shield finally gave, and he pushed me behind him, right before three people fired at me." He sobbed. "His shield was already gone. Why did he do that? He's a brilliant scientist, and I'm just a shitty bartender in debt out my ass."

Leti wrapped the man in his arms. "You're Sebastian, right?"

"Yeah, so?"

"Verion felt really bad about not being able to save Nina. He really liked her, and she died helping him."

"He told me that. What does it matter?"

"I only knew him a few days, but I know that he was worried for your safety. He wanted to make up for Nina, to make sure the person she cared most for was safe. That's the kind of man he was."

"He was far more valuable than me."

"Don't be an idiot," Leti said, voice growing hard. "Life is precious no matter what. He chose to give his for you. Don't drown in the what-ifs."

Sebastian leaned his head on Leti's shoulder.

"You're right. Sorry for my blubbering. Who are you anyway?"

Leti smiled softly through his tears. "I'm the captain's mate. I'm guessing you're our new crewmember, right? How do you feel about llamas?"

Hack watched as his mate comforted a stranger, despite his own grief. Leti had known Morrick more within a few days than his colleagues likely had in twenty years. The two survivors stood behind the kneeling men, guarding Leti. Hack had a feeling his mate had just gained two bodyguards, which meant two more crew for him.

Cas threw an arm around Hack's shoulders. "That is one damn amazing mate you have there, Will. You sure he's yours and not mine? He deserves the better-looking brother."

Dru growled as he elbowed Cas in the gut. "That's our captain's mate, asshole. Back off. He's ours."

"Dru, beautiful Dru." Cas turned his flirty eyes on Hack's lieutenant. He paused, puzzled by the sight of Monty perched on her head. "Who's that lizard on your head? Does Lerais know you've been claimed by another?"

"Well, he will when he realizes the damn thing sleeps on my pillow. I can't get rid of him." She reached up and rubbed the newt's little head. "He's growing on me though."

"Hack," Audre said, long legs striding through the battlefield. "The spaceport guards said they will clean this up. We're free to go."

"Good, we need to get moving," he said.

"Wait, Will," Leti said. He joined Hack's group, pulling Sebastian with him. "Since I imagine we killed several crews here, we need to check the docked Concord ships. Remember, Lilah said that they keep prisoners on board for amusement?"

"Yeah, we do need to do that." Hack sighed, hugging his mate tightly to him. "Dru, do you have word on Morgan?"

"Nettle said that he has a concussion, but he should be fine when he wakes. The others are being tended to, but nothing life-threatening."

"Cas, Audre, can you all assist us in checking over the Concord ships? If it's anything like the one we saw, they'll have several prisoners on board. We'll need help with transporting them."

"Of course, Hack," Audre said. "I'll start arranging it. You take care of our wounded."

"We need to bring Morrick with us, Will," Leti said softly. "I want his son to be able to see him one last time. Please?"

"Of course, baby," Hack answered. "We'll put him in a cryo chamber."

"Okay." He frowned at the blood that seeped from Hack's wounds. "Let's get you to the med bay. Sebastian, will you take him? You need to get checked over too. Follow Juniper over there and he'll show you the ship."

He pushed and prodded Hack until he agreed to go with the other man. "Dru and I will handle things here."

Hack sighed and gave in to his mate, ignoring Cas's laughter as he limped away.

"Oh, and identify yourself before getting on the ship," Dru said. "I left two guards."

"We had two more people to spare?" Hack asked.

"Two more survivors wanted to fight, but were too injured. Another's in the pilot seat."

"Damn it," he muttered, reluctantly impressed. His ship was only so big, and his crew kept expanding.

***

LETI COULDN'T STOP his tears from falling, but Dru and he made sure that Morrick's body was taken back to the ship, then they checked over the wounded, directing them to the right people. The spaceport guards had lost two men, The Yellow Solace one, and, of course, The Blue Solace lost Morrick. Almost every person who fought was injured in some way, keeping the medical officers busy.

Leti checked on Princess, who had shrunk back to one foot, his traveling size. He picked him up and draped him around his neck. "You did well today, Princess. Daddy loves you."

"I think we all love that dragon now," Draif said. "By the way, I'm wearing your lucky baby bunny sweater on the next mission."

Leti laughed half-heartedly. "It really is lucky." He pushed his face into Draif's shoulder. "I should have made Verion wear it."

"Hey, now. It's okay, Leti." Draif rocked him in his arms. "His death is shit, there's no getting around that. It's okay to grieve."

"He was so excited, Draif. He was going to call his son when all this was over and talk to him, forge a relationship."

"I'm so sorry, Leti," he said. "Gods, there is nothing I can say or do to make this better. We'll deal, okay? You aren't alone. You have me and the crew of The Blue Solace. You have your kids, all eight hundred of them. You have Wobble and Princess Buttercup. You have your mate, Leti. Your mate who loves you so damn much. We'll all be with you here. We'll all grieve together."

"We'll make them pay, Leti," Cas said from behind him. Leti knew he was Hack's brother, but he hadn't really met him yet. The large blue Grell nodded to him. "You have all of Charybdis Station behind you, Leti. We'll make the Concords pay for this."

Leti nodded, misery lessoning a little. "Did you find any prisoners on board the Concord ships?"

Cas's face was grim. "Yeah, between twenty and thirty-five in each. All non-human or human hybrids. We're getting them medical attention now, and Union Station's helping to sort who's who. If they have somewhere to go, we'll get them there. If they don't, they have a home with us back at the station."

"Thank you, Cas," Leti said.

"You and Draif here are family now, Leti. You don't know the lengths we'll go for our family."

LETI WATCHED as Morrick's body gradually covered

with ice, freezing in the cryo chamber. Hack's arms wrapped around him, warming him. His mate hadn't let him out of his sight once he got back to the ship.

Verion's plain face frosted over with a finality that hit Leti suddenly. He turned in Hack's arms, sobbing. His mate rubbed his back and held him close. There was nothing that would make this better. Leti knew Verion would never see his son again. The last words spoken between them would be angry and hurtful.

Sebastian stood silently next to them, eyes full of emotion but quiet. Leti knew he still felt guilty, and nothing anyone said seemed to make him feel any better.

Of course, Dr. Olivia Franklin didn't help matters. "Such a brilliant mind gone, and for what? To save some worthless hybrid?"

Sebastian gasped, tears escaping down his cheeks.

"Shut the fuck up, bitch," Dru said. "You're still with us because you may be of use at the station, but I swear to the gods, you spout your pro-human purity bullshit one more time and I'll put my phaser to your head. Got it?"

Franklin's lips pursed like she had just sucked a lemon. She simply turned and walked away. Princess hissed and snapped at her as she passed him, causing the woman to jump and run out the door.

"What do we do now, Captain?" Draif stood on the other side of Sebastian, arm around his shoulder, offering what comfort he could.

"Most of the survivors from the other ships don't have homes. The Yellow Solace and The Green Solace are transporting them back to Charybdis Station. We'll travel with them, keeping together." He looked around at his crew. They gathered around the body of a fallen client turned friend. Each pet sat next to its person, offering unconditional love and acceptance. The animals were part of the crew now too, offering aid in different ways, helping to hold everyone together.

"From what Nina told me, this artifact has the potential to destroy whole worlds," Sebastian said.

"We do what Morrick set out to do. We figure out what the hell this artifact is, and then we keep it from falling into the wrong hands," Hack said.

Each member of his crew nodded in agreement. One at a time, they left the room, patting Sebastian and Leti on the shoulders or offering hugs.

Eventually, Leti and Hack were all that were left. Hack hugged him close and kissed the top of his head. "I love you, mate. You amaze me with your empathy, your bravery, and your kindness."

"I love you too, Will. I told you, you're stuck with me now. I'm yours forever."

"We'll figure this out, love. We'll make things right."

EPILOGUE

*L*eti sat at his desk, multiple screens pulled up and Morrick's notes spread out in front of him. Pepper cooed from her carrier next to him, and Rizzie played in the corner with a few of the other child survivors.

He tried to make sense of Morrick's notes and what he knew of the horrific history of the Crellic System, but he kept coming back to the words written repetitively throughout the pages in front of him: *artifact's reaction to necrosis.* Death and the Crellic System were not topics Leti wanted to think of together, but he had the sinking feeling that they were key in understanding the element.

He pushed away the notes and looked at one of the screens, message ready to send. He had hesitated all day to send this, but he knew it was the right thing to do. What he didn't know were the consequences of his actions. Maybe he shouldn't interfere, but if he was in the other man's shoes, he would want to know.

He hit send, then turned to watch Rizzie and her friends. He placed a hand on his belly, thinking of the little peanut that grew within him. Right now, the ship was full of life, the crewmembers, the pets, the survivors. Voices and laughter came from the hall and Biscuit and Porkchop ran in the door, heading to the children. Princess snored on the bed, head on Hack's favorite pillow. The only dark spot in all the light around him lay in the cold of the cyro chamber.

My beloved son,

Two days ago, you were born, and I wasn't there. I was in my office, researching the Chelieac disease. When I checked my missed calls, I saw your face for the first time, and I fell in love. Your little nose was smooshed up and you looked so angry, wailing about your hunger. Your mother laughed at you and kissed your head, holding you close to her breast. I wasn't there. I couldn't hold you, feel your soft skin and kiss your brown curls. I wasn't there, but I love you more than I ever thought I could love anyone or anything.

I want to make the galaxy an amazing place for you. I want to make sure you never get sick, never suffer, and never feel any pain. I know I will likely never send you this letter. Who writes letters anyway, right? I will keep working from the moment I rise to the moment I go to sleep. I may never hold you as often as I want to, but sometimes, when I think of you, late at night, I will write to you. Maybe, when you are old enough to read, I'll show them to you. We can read them together and I can hug you close to me.

I love you more than all the stardust in the galaxy.

-- Your father

The Blue Solace Series – science fiction/fantasy, mpreg

- The Mercenary's Mate
- The General's Mate
- The Soldier's Mate
- The Lieutenant's Mate
- The Engineer's Mate
- The Captain's Mate
- The Rebel's Mate – *Coming Soon*
- Fire's Mate – *Coming Soon*

The Hobson Hills Omegas – non-shifter, mpreg, omegaverse

- Falling for the Omega
- Snow Kisses for My Omega
- Romancing the Omega
- Healing the Omega
- A Pint for my Omega
- Unraveling the Omega
- The Alpha's Christmas Wish

Hobson Hills Shorts – short stories from the world of Hobson Hills Omegas

- The Beta's Love Song

• Bennett's Dream

• Justin's Journey

• Grey's Gift

• Hobson Hills Shorts: Volume One

The Silver Isles – paranormal, mermen, mpreg

• The Guppy Prince

• The Not so Little Merman – *Coming Soon*

• The Sea Witch – *Coming Soon*

If you would like to keep up with releases, please like and follow me on Instagram (@c.w._gray) or Facebook (@cwgrayauthor), join C.W. Gray's Reading Nook on Facebook, or visit my website at https://cwgray-author.com.